NIGHT VARMINTS

A KITTY ADVENTURE #2

NIGHT VARMINTS

A KITTY ADVENTURE #2

DONNA MAE SMITH

Library of Congress Control Number:2019913270

ISBN: 979-1981191215

This is a tale of fiction and fictional characters. Any similarity to real persons or pets, living or passed on, is accidental and of no intention of the author.

EDITED

BY

JANET CRUDELE

ILLUSTRATIONS

BY

DONNA MAE SMITH

DEDICATIONS

TO

DADDY
STANLEY GRIGELIS

I LOVE BEING A
WATERMAN'S DAUGHTER

&

DARRELL RAY

THANKS FOR THE HUBBY SUPPORT!
YOU ARE A GREAT DAD
TO OUR FUR BABIES!

CONTENTS

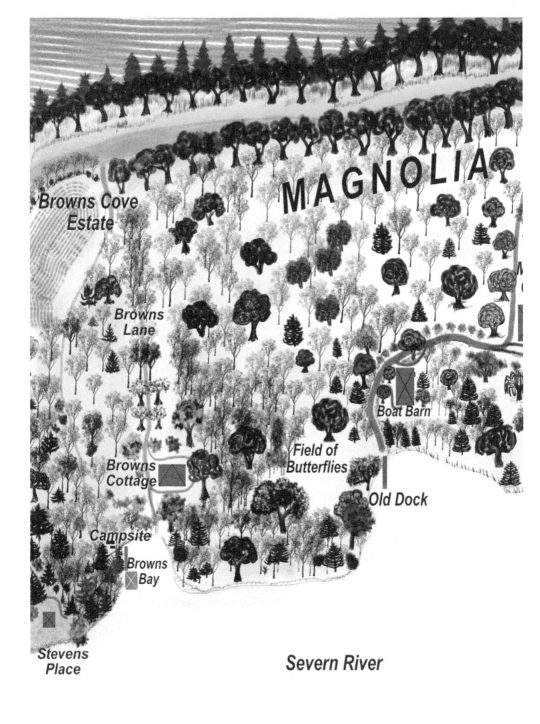

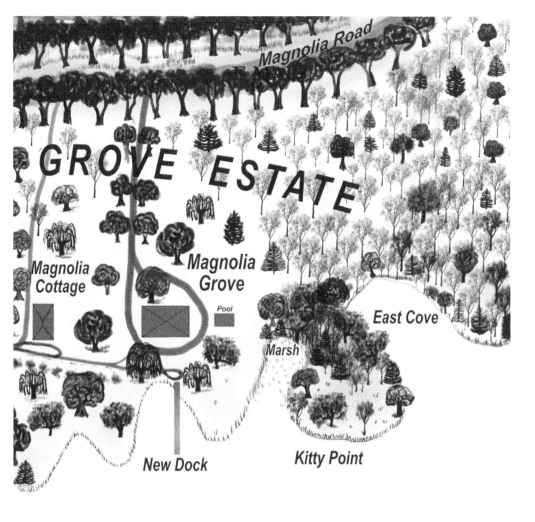

Magnolia Road

GROVE ESTATE

Magnolia
Cottage

Magnolia
Grove

Pool

East Cove

Marsh

New Dock

Kitty Point

Hidden Cove

Rabbit Forest

1 ~ NIGHT LIGHTS

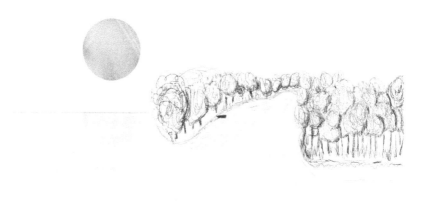

Kitty enjoys a still and quiet night

The night is clear, and the moon sits high in the sky. Its full moonlight reflects and glistens off the calm water of Virginia's Severn River and Mobjack Bay. It is indeed a fine evening for enjoying the water, the twinkling night-lights, and the crisp air.

This is a majestic piece of land. It points towards the mouth of the Severn River and into Mobjack Bay. It is also a haven for wildlife. The westside of the Point is a marshland cove. Many birds and turtles visit or raise families there. On the eastside of the Point is a large water cove where animals congregate from the air, the land, and the sea. They hunt, bathe in the sun, and assemble for meetings.

This is Kitty's favorite spot. Here he spends much of his time playing, socializing, and exploring. The Point is impossible to see from land. Kitty discovered it while exploring the edge of the woods. There, Kitty found a thin, low path winding through the thick forest. He soon learned the path is the smaller animals' secret road in and out of the Point.

Kitty has only lived on land a few weeks, for he was born at sea. He and Momma went on a long voyage with Captain and his nephew, Rod, on the big boat Betty. They traveled from Mexico to Florida, and then back to Virginia's Mobjack Bay. Here, on the Severn River, is where Kitty now calls home.

Kitty is the newcomer to the neighborhood. However, he is a social and gregarious cat, so he has been very busy getting to know the many residents. He enjoys having so many friends.

Tonight, Kitty sits on the Point and looks out over the river. At first, the night is seemingly still and quiet. But soon, Kitty hears a raccoon cleaning his fish at the water's edge. He purrs and chatters about his good luck.

The quiet sound of chirping crickets surrounds Kitty. However, the occasional hoot from the resident owl family loudly and clearly breaks the silence.

From the east, the humming sound of a boat departs the Mobjack Bay and enters the mouth of the Severn River. It is a familiar and relaxing sound on the water, easy to fall asleep with and easy to sleep through.

The boat, the clear night, and the twinkling stars bring memories of recent sea adventures. Kitty falls into a dreamy state and into a memory of North Carolina when they moored the big boat Betty at the Cape Lookout Bight. That beautiful and calm bay had the best sea turtles, wild ponies, and lighthouse in North Carolina. His memories are about to turn into pleasant dreams.

As if the night is too quiet or too lacking in adventure, a flash from across the river interrupts Kitty's nostalgic stupor. His eyes open wide, and he springs to his feet. "What is that?"

Breaking the silence of the night, the flare pops, and bangs, then it arches high in the sky to drop warning into the Severn River.

Kitty's head begins to tilt back and forth. *A flare is supposed to mean emergency. Even if there is an emergency, it seems strange to see an emergency flare on the calm river tonight. The night is quiet, and sound carries well over calm water. Still nights make yells for help loud.*

The sound of a boat nears. *Maybe that boat is heading to rescue whoever sent up that flare?*

After several minutes, the slow-moving boat comes into Kitty's view. It is a fishing trawler typically used for commercial fishing. There are no lights in the cabin or bow.

They are good at using the moonlight to steer, Kitty notes.

Instead of the boat crossing the river towards the location of the flare and the hidden cove, it heads towards the Point. Directly in front of Kitty, the boat comes to a stop. Kitty hears the splosh of the boat's anchor going overboard. The boat then pulls forward until the anchor holds.

Kitty's keen eyesight observes the trawler. *The man outside in the bow is short but very stocky.*

Some quick movements from inside the cabin catches Kitty's attention. *That must be the trawler's captain inside the cabin.*

Well, that boat is not saving anyone tonight. Maybe they just need to anchor for a night's sleep. He watches closely but sees no further movement.

Kitty knows a lot about being on the water. He has spent many nights on the big boat Betty, often watching Captain secure her anchor. *If they are spending the night, they have not anchored that boat very securely.*

All is quiet again. Both men on the trawler sit very still. Kitty intensely thinks and observes. He then realizes that the men are too quiet. *They certainly are not preparing the boat to stay overnight. They are not even speaking. What are they waiting for?*

Kitty immediately receives an answer. From across the river, a small boat engine starts. Kitty can hear it come onto the river, even from that distance. He listens more closely.

Alarm sets in. Kitty realizes the small boat is slowly heading towards the Point.

It is coming this way!

The boat sounds like it is struggling to cross the river. Kitty begins to pace back and forth, never taking his eyes off either boat. His face frowns in concern.

I have a very bad feeling about this.

Long moments drag into what feels like suspension in time. Finally, a flat bottom boat, a skiff, comes into view. A skiff is well suited for use on Virginia's rivers. Unlike a V shape hull design, a skiff's flat bottom allows maneuvering in very shallow waters. In addition, skiffs easily push on and off sandy, grassy, muddy, or marshy shores.

This skiff slowly steers towards the anchored trawler. It turns around and docks on the port side, which, to Kitty's good fortune, happens to be the side Kitty is facing.

Kitty sees two men on the skiff and starts taking mental notes. One is a tall man with a black hat. The other man is much shorter and has a long, full beard.

That skiff sure is sitting low in the water. Ah! Well, look at that! It has a heavy load of crates on it.

The two men in the skiff begin passing crates to the two men on the trawler. They try to be quiet, but they grunt and groan from the heavy work. Kitty hears an occasional whisper.

He also notices one of the owls drop quietly from a high tree branch. It soars down to a tree closer to the water. Kitty sees it is one of his alliances, Mr. Owl.

Kitty befriended Mrs. Owl the first night Kitty found the Point. Since then, Mr. and Mrs. Owl and Kitty have come to an agreement. If Kitty tells them where the best and tastiest mice are, in trade, the Owls will not attack nor eat Kitty. In addition, they allow him access to the Point's grassy area, Kitty's favorite new spot to explore, play, hunt mice, and think.

Mr. and Mrs. Owl may even help Kitty from time to time. They never said that yet, but Kitty is very wishful about that part.

What Kitty does not realize is that Mrs. Owl has taken a fancy to him. She finds that "Master Kitty is intelligent and uniquely respectful to everyone and everything he encounters."

Mrs. Owl recently told Mr. Owl, "He is a special child, Papa. I predict that one day he will be very important to Magnolia Grove. Master Kitty has our protection."

One rule clearly stands. When Mrs. Owl speaks, all listen.

Naturally, owls catch and eat small animals. To best protect Kitty, the wise birds develop a plan to ensure that Kitty keeps his instinctive fear and respect of predator birds. For now, Kitty must work hard to earn passage through Mr. and Mrs. Owl's territory.

Of course, the Owls already know where the best mice are, but the agreement they have with Kitty keeps him very busy. And Mrs. Owl can keep an eye on him.

Kitty looks up at Mr. Owl sitting as close to the boats as the trees allow. *That is not a very good spot for him to hunt. Mr. Owl must be watching those boats, too.*

Kitty's focus returns to the men moving the crates. Suddenly, as they are transferring one of the crates off the skiff, it slips out of the gloves of the man with the black hat and into the gloves of the short and stocky crew member from the trawler. He drops it. Onto the deck the crate loudly "Thumps!"

Horrors of echoes resound over the water.

The men freeze, and Kitty senses their fear. The captain in the trawler's cabin, still hidden from view, yells as loud as a whisper can yell. "What are you three doing out there? Are you trying to wake everyone on the river and bring unwanted attention? You do realize the danger of that, yes?"

Kitty files the voice of the trawler's captain deep into his memory. *I will remember him. That voice sounds very mean.*

Hearing the resonating sound of the echoing thumps, nearby birds wake, squawk, and fly away. That, in turn, stirs smaller brush residents. Within seconds, raccoons, rabbits, skunks, squirrels, and others gather at the forest edge. Soon, a mother deer, Miss Doe, steps out of the forest and peers at the boats, the men, and Kitty.

"Kitty, what woke me?"

"I think they are varmints, Miss Doe, human varmints!"

After relocating the crates onto the trawler, the men breathe with exhaustion. They are unaware of the many observers now witnessing the night's main event.

The men and their suspicious behavior make Kitty realize this group must be hiding something. *They think no one can see them and that everyone is asleep.*

Kitty can see the many animals observing from land. He also sees many creatures observing from the river. They all have similar questions while staring at the strange boats and their newest friend. Many of them have never seen people or boats so close. Many have never seen people at all.

Wise Mr. and Mrs. Great Horned Owl have been watching everything from their nearby perch.

Kitty moves as close as possible to the water's edge. He goes on self-appointed guard duty. "Meow, meow, I will protect all of you!"

From a distance, Mrs. Owl smiles at Kitty's bravery. She sits high in a tree several trees back from Mr. Owl. She watches and listens to Kitty and the men.

"These crates with all this evidence are soon gone," laughs the short stocky man from the fishing trawler.

The presumed captain from inside the trawler's cabin, barks in a loud whisper, "Shut up. You have caused enough trouble. How many times do I have to remind you that water carries sound well?"

Evidence must be a very bad thing, Kitty decides.

The moonlight now catches the fourth man. His hair is white in color, wild in design, and shaped like a ball. *The man with the white hair belching orders must be the captain.* Kitty further thinks, *I sure am glad I have my Captain!*

After a few minutes of rest, the man with the black hat starts his skiff's engine. His partner with the long, full, beard stays on the varmint trawler. He will get a ride home later because he stays to help unload the cargo on a secret barge out in the Mobjack Bay. The trawler slowly turns east.

Kitty begins to feel agitated. *Momma said I might one day face a human varmint. But there is a boatload of varmints heading out to sea.* In a desperate act, Kitty turns to the remaining skiff and its lone passenger for possible answers.

The skiff does not head across the river from where it came. Instead, and luckily for Kitty, it crosses the mouth of the cove and continues up the Severn River towards Captain's big dock and home.

Kitty starts running. He runs as hard as he can, using the winding animal path under the brush. He thinks all the way. *I must beat him to the New Dock.*

Those human varmints are moving Evidence! Evidence? What is Evidence? Who owns that skiff? I need to know where that thing is going!

Kitty clears the woods and looks towards Captain's New Dock. *That skiff is going to pass the pier and keep heading upriver.* He races to cross their wide stretch of lawn.

Avoiding the curvy shoreline's path, Kitty cuts through the woodlands area leading to the Old Dock. *This route will be shorter than following the shore and bend in the river. If I can get to the Old Dock first, I may be able to see or hear where that skiff is heading.*

Kitty races behind the Boat Barn where the dirt lane curves towards the Old Dock and reaches the end of the Old Dock before the varmint boat passes.

The skiff travels very close to the shore and appears to head straight towards the Old Dock. Kitty drops down on the planks as low as he can.

Kitty freezes in place, and his eyes open wide. *Is that varmint coming HERE?*

The skiff soon reaches the end of the Old Dock. However, it does not stop. *I am so glad it is not coming this way, but where is it going? Oh no, is he going to see me?*

The skiff passes so close to the pier that the man with the black hat reaches out and touches the end as he goes by. He does not even notice Kitty hunkering down at the end of the dock.

Kitty detects a kind of plastic smell as the skiff passes. He also hears the man singing a tune.

"A wise old owl lived in an oak.

The more he heard, the less he spoke.

The less he spoke, the more he heard!

Why aren't we all like that wise old bird?"

The tall man with the black hat does not notice that Kitty closely observes him from the end of the Old Dock.

That tall man in the black hat sure does not seem to be very wise. He does not see too good, either.

The skiff continues close to the shore and passes more forest belonging to Magnolia Grove. *If that skiff goes much farther upriver, I may never find it.* Kitty contemplates his options of getting a ride by boat, traveling upriver along the shoreline, or possibly using the road in front of Magnolia Grove Estate. *Momma says I mustn't go on the road.*

Suddenly, as if Kitty willed it, the skiff turns starboard into the next cove. The engine suddenly cuts, and Kitty relaxes a bit. He smiles. *I have you now.*

That is not so very far away, Kitty first thinks. Momma said that Magnolia Grove Estate goes to the next cove. He realizes he has never been into the west woods.

Kitty has only been as far as the wooded edge of the Field of Butterflies. His first friend on land, mean and grouchy MadmanMax, had once told Kitty to go there to find tasty mice to eat. At that time, Kitty was younger, lost, and very hungry.

But MadmanMax is not that mean, just grouchy. MadmanMax befriended Kitty and helped him find food, shelter, and Captain's sister, Miss Grace.

~

Not too long ago, very early in the morning, Kitty broke the rules and snuck off Betty to play. He then fell asleep under a tree. When he awoke, Betty was gone. Kitty did not know where he was and found himself marooned at the Old Dock.

When Captain discovered Kitty was not on Betty, he had no time to return for him. Captain had to get to the US Naval Academy in Annapolis to give the new school year's opening ceremony speech.

Captain knew Kitty would find protection with Grace.

~

Kitty thinks his situation over. *There are many more woods between here and that cove. This is all I am going to discover tonight. I need daylight to find more.*

Kitty has never been so tired. Excited, he shouts, "Tomorrow I go to that cove!"

Kitty shakes off the desire to nap on the Old Dock and heads home. He yawns a big yawn. *There is no need to worry everyone by me falling asleep here. Anyway, Momma will be mad if I stay outside too late. I think I am going to have a lot of explaining to do.*

Kitty walks very sluggish and yawns repeatedly. It is a much longer walk home tonight than usual. Finally, Kitty enters the house, happy to be heading to his room.

Even as tired as Kitty is, he notices it is a grand room. He and Momma are lucky to have a view that overlooks the river, the pier, the big boat Betty, and Captain's racing sailboat. They even have their own private bathroom with mirrors and glass.

Kitty jumps up on his bed and cuddles next to sleeping Momma. She opens her eyes, mutters that he is late, purrs, and goes back to sleep.

Kitty thinks over his adventure. *I bet everyone is going to be surprised to find out we have human varmints!*

Kitty falls asleep murmuring, "I knew adventures on land would be exiting!"

"Meow, I must go upriver and chase some varmints. You
stay close to the house today, Miss Grace, until I get home!"

Most mornings, Captain and his sister, Grace, gather in his kitchen at Magnolia Grove. They have breakfast and discuss Captain's business affairs before Grace begins her workday. Magnolia Grove Estate is very large, with two homes, two docks, a large Boat Barn, and over two miles of Severn River frontage.

This morning, Grace is more concerned about Kitty. She seriously looks at her brother. "Sam, Kitty did not come over to visit this morning. Nor did he make it to the bus stop. Kitty has not missed seeing Billy off to school since he first arrived here. Sam, is Kitty home?"

Grace's youngest son, Billy, catches the bus to school during the week. Billy was Kitty's first human friend he made on land. Billy is from the city, so Kitty taught Billy how to live in the country. Billy never liked the outdoors before Kitty came to Magnolia Grove.

Kitty likes Billy very much, but Billy is still very young. Unlike Rod, Billy's older brother, Billy is not good at going to sea or finding adventure.

Captain laughs. "Yes, Kitty is still in bed and snoring hard. Maybe last night he had too much fun with all those animals he hangs out with in the woods. I told you the Point would be a healthy and safe place to play for a smart boy like Kitty."

Grace sighs in relief. "Well, I am glad he is here. I was a bit worried because that little boy sure can get into some mischief. Of course, the rest of the time he is eating or sleeping." They both laugh.

Captain continues with a bit of loving irritation in his voice. "I know that to be true. We have been home only a few weeks, and I have had to clean up a gallon of paint in the barn, pick up every screw and bolt I own, and reorganize every shelf. Oh yes, and I had to replace the kitchen cat door."

Grace replies, "I feel sorry for you! You do also realize I came home and found my entire yarn collection scattered in other rooms. Hundreds of balls of yarn tied together and strung throughout the house! Obviously, yarn makes fun toys for Kitty."

Captain laughs. "Well, Grace, you better keep that crochet room door shut. It is simply too much temptation for Kitty. He cannot help himself. Oh, and as a warning, and from experience, I would not leave a bag of flour within his reach either."

Captain proceeds to tell Grace how Kitty discovered flour aboard Betty. "He had the best time sliding all over the kitchen and turning it, and himself, as white as the flour. He made an awful mess, and it took hours to clean."

Grace shakes her head yes in full agreement. "Oh my, Captain, I know that was a sticky mess to clean up."

"Yes, it was especially hard to clean out of the corners and cracks. The flour was much worse than the milk spill. At least with the milk, Momma Sara and Kitty could drink up most of the mess before I had to start cleaning. On Betty, Sara spent a lot of her time cleaning up after Kitty. He is a messy son."

Grace responds in laughter, "Just in case, I will batten down the hatches!"

Captain looks at his sister with humorous confusion. "Until Kitty moved in, you never cared for a cat. It amazes me how close you and he are, Grace. He always seems to be guarding you."

Grace smiles tenderly. She knows Kitty is her guardian. "Sam, my youngest, says Kitty thinks I am not able to take care of myself. After all, I almost let a coyote kill me. It is still amazing every time I remember how a very young cat came to my rescue. That brave boy risked his life to save me. Me! Someone that did not want him or like him. Kitty taught me a valuable lesson that day."

Captain looks at his sister's face and melts into a look of deep understanding. "Yes, Kitty and Sara are both very special cats, very special cats, indeed, Grace."

Captain and Grace are still chuckling over Kitty as they continue to discuss Captain's schedule, bills to pay, and various repairs and work needed on the estate.

"We better get the Boat Barn roof redone before the winter storms set in, Grace. The last storm ripped off some old shingles, and the barn is leaking in several places. Who do we have available?"

"I will call around town for estimates and schedules."

"That is great. I also need to go to the post office this morning. While I am out, Grace, do you need anything?"

"Oh yes, I would appreciate it if you would drive upriver to Miss Brown's house and pick up our order of three dozen eggs. She also has your repaired jeans. You and Betty are hard on work clothes."

"Your wish is my command, dear Sister," Captain replies.

Grace chuckles, "You would drive to the other side of the county for Hope Brown's flavorful eggs."

"That is true. She must feed those chickens something special, because they are the best eggs I have ever tasted."

Grace stops. "Oh yes, Sam, I just remembered something that may be worth an enquiry. Miss Brown hired her brother from the Washington D.C. area to rebuild her old boathouse and repair the pier decking. Maybe he replaces roofs, too. His company is already here with tools and equipment."

"Miss Brown did not hire local workers? It seems expensive to bring in an outside company, even if it is her brother."

"Yes, that is true. However, luck has it that her brother and a few of his friends wanted a fishing vacation. They are using Hope Brown's place as a base camp and as a jobsite. They brought a big truck with equipment and a motor home to cook and sleep in. You can check them out while over there. In the meantime, I will call some local companies."

"Will do, Grace. That certainly is worth asking about. Also, are Billy and Rod joining us next weekend for our Annual Shoreline Cleanup Day?"

"Yes, both boys will be joining you. We will all have a big breakfast Saturday, 6:00 a.m. sharp. And no worries, for we will get more of Miss Brown's tasty eggs."

"That sounds like a great start for the day, Grace." Captain gives his sister a shoulder hug and then pats his belly. "I can taste breakfast already! I am so glad you are here!"

"You mean you are glad I am here to cook for you! How did you manage before I arrived?" Grace lovingly hits her brother on the shoulder.

Captain smiles and looks at Grace with sincere admiration. He has great confidence in his sister, and he is very relieved to have her run Magnolia Grove Estate. Not only is she a great cook, but her management skills save him money and a lot of worry. Grace is the best person possible to manage his business.

~

Grace and her husband owned a small marina in Maryland. After she lost her husband, her world fell apart. Captain wanted his sister and family closer. He offered Grace and her two boys, Rod and Billy, a home at Magnolia Cottage, the original home on the estate.

Captain had wanted to build a new home anyway, so he built Magnolia Grove next door. Grace sold her marina and moved her family to Virginia and into Magnolia Cottage. She then began her important position of managing her brother's estate and personal affairs. It has turned out to be one of the best decisions she ever made.

Grace adores her brother, Sam. He helped her boys adjust to the loss of their father and helped them adapt to a new life.

~

Captain continues his excitement for the Annual Shoreline Cleanup Day. "Grace, it will be educational for Billy to help gather trash. He will see for himself and learn of the problems that marine pollution causes the river, wildlife, and people. Billy will begin to understand the importance of having safe and clean water. He can learn why all of us need to live a life rich with environmental awareness."

Grace nods her head with approval.

"Most of us along the river clean our own shoreline. However, with so much trash, such as Styrofoam, plastic and cans washing onto the shores, it can be difficult for many landowners, especially seniors or those without a boat. Much of the waterfrontage has marshland or swamp that makes it difficult to reach by foot to clean. Those areas are only accessible by boat.

Three years ago, a few of us started extending our personal cleanup to neighbors in need knowing it would benefit us all. We started with five boats."

Grace sees her brother's face beam with pride as he continues. "You know, Grace, people here really care about the water. This year, we have over fifty boats signed up for the event."

Captain gets a little serious sounding. "Many of these families have made their living on these local waters for generations. I am happy to use my little bit of knowledge and resources to help this wonderful area. Our river will soon be looking as clean as your kitchen, Grace."

She laughs, "That is a funny one, Sam. Your little bit of knowledge is plenty, and you know it! The residents here are lucky to have you as a part of the community. And, for your information, nothing you ever do will look as clean as my kitchen!" She giggles as she sips her coffee.

Kitty bounces into the room. "Meow, meow, I sure am hungry!" He dives into his food bowl and begins gobbling down breakfast. Kitty is so excited that he keeps on meowing and talking while spreading his food two feet out in all directions.

"Meow…Good morning, Captain…Meow…Good morning, Miss Grace… Where is Momma? I have a… a big day… today… a real big day… Meow…Varmints, Captain… we got varmints, and… meow!"

Grace looks alarmed. "Sam, something seems to have Kitty very excited."

She speaks softly. "Kitty, slow down. Have you talked to Momma? When I came over here, I left Momma Sara sleeping in Rod's bed. Who knows where she is sleeping by now!"

Captain watches Kitty with great curiosity. "OK, Kitty, everything is all right now. Eat your breakfast. If you want, you can go with me on errands and tell me all about your problems."

Captain cannot help but grin as he continues. "First, we will go to town and the post office. When we come back, we will run upriver to the Brown Estate for some eggs and the mending. You have yet to go upriver, Kitty. Would you like that?"

Kitty stops and thinks about the word. "Upriver, you say? Upriver! Yes, Captain, meow, I need to go upriver!"

"We will leave soon. See if Momma wants to join us."

Kitty calms a bit with a full belly and jumps into Grace's lap. "Meow, I missed you and Billy this morning. Meow, I am sorry. I was very busy last night, meow."

Kitty gently paws Grace on the face. "Meow, do not worry about me today. I must go upriver, meow, and chase down some varmints. You stay close to the house today, Miss Grace. Meow! You must stay close to the house until I get home!" Kitty protectively warns her as he pets her face.

"Are you trying to say you are my protector? You are so good to me, Kitty." Grace gives Kitty a hug and puts him on the floor. "I am going to clean up your room now. You find Momma and go have fun with Captain Sam."

Grace leaves the room, and Kitty follows to ensure she is on her regular routine of caring for the houses and estate. *Miss Grace is safe, and she will be busy for hours.* Kitty runs next door.

Kitty enters through the cat door that Rod's dog, Bear, now uses. He finds Momma sleeping on Rod's bed. *This used to be Momma's room. Then, before I was born, Momma and Captain moved next door into the new house, Magnolia Grove.*

Kitty jumps onto Rod's bed and starts pouncing up and down beside Momma. She unwillingly wakes, stretching her legs out far in front of her and opening her paws wide.

Kitty shouts, "Momma, we must go chase varmints. They are upriver. They are trouble, Momma. I can smell it!"

"What are you going on about, Kitty? What varmints?"

"Captain is taking me upriver, Momma. He wants to know if you want to go with us. Let us go, Momma!

We have human varmints, Momma, human varmints! Get up, please, Momma. We must find them upriver!"

"Kitty, are you telling me Captain is going upriver so both of you can look for human varmints?"

"Yes Momma," Kitty replies in absolute truth, truth as he sees it anyway.

"Kitty, I want you to calm down and tell me everything from the beginning."

"We must hurry Momma. Captain is waiting. Do you want to go with us?"

"I better go, so I can keep an eye on you two. And somebody needs to explain to me what was so important that you slept through our morning lessons and walking Billy to the bus stop."

They both make their way back to the kitchen to wait for Captain. While Momma eats a sardine snack, Kitty explains the two boats meeting in the cove and the four men transporting the heavy crates from the skiff to the fishing trawler.

Momma thinks the story over. "Kitty, you do make an adventure out of everything. Maybe they were working and just fishing or crabbing."

"No, Momma, no, they are varmints! They were moving something called Evidence and they dropped it. When they dropped it…"

Captain peeks into the kitchen. "Is everybody ready to go? The morning rain is about to end. Load up!"

Captain yells out to Grace, "Remember Billy will not be coming home on the bus. I will pick him up after band practice."

"OK," Grace cheerfully replies.

Momma Sara quickly moves towards Captain's truck.

Kitty follows and then loudly states, "But Momma, you are not listening. They are human varmints!" He follows behind her, muttering "I will show Momma. I will find those human varmints again myself!"

Captain, Sara, and Kitty load into the truck and begin the ride to town. Captain rolls down the window for Kitty to catch the wind, and Captain and Sara start talking. They seemingly forget about Kitty's important mission.

Captain looks concerned. "Sara, what is bothering Kitty? He is more upset this morning than ever before."

"Oh Captain, he saw two boats on the river last night that upset him. A skiff had one tall man with a black hat and one short man with a long, full beard. There were two others on a trawler. They all moved some crates from the skiff to the trawler.

Kitty now believes the river, the animals, and all of us are in the gravest of danger. I do not know Captain. He seems certain, but you know what an imagination he has."

Captain replies, "Yes, he does conjure up frequent trouble. He is a smart boy, our Kitty, but he is young, and we must keep a close watch on him."

"Yes, he is young," repeats Sara. "Meow, Kitty."

"I am grown, Momma. I can take care of myself," Kitty pouts. "I am going to find those human varmints and that Evidence they are hiding at night."

"Momma, what is Evidence? I can tell it is bad."

"Evidence is not always bad. For example, your crates might be full of something good. Therefore, the crates would prove good evidence.

Do you understand, Kitty? Not all evidence is proof that gets people in trouble or punished, or even put in jail."

Kitty gets excited. "Those men on the trawler were afraid of the crates, Momma. I am going to find that evidence and prove we have bad human varmints upriver."

Momma smiles and reports to Captain. "Kitty says he is going to find the evidence and prove we have bad human varmints upriver."

Kitty does not understand the great importance of Momma and Captain's relationship. Momma happens to be one of the very few cats in the world that can talk to humans. Momma and

Captain protect this secret, trying to keep it just between themselves.

Captain laughs. "So, our Kitty said he is going to find the hidden evidence and save us all, huh?" Captain then thinks a bit. "Now Sara, where do you think Kitty learned the word evidence?"

"That is a good question, Captain."

Momma looks to Kitty for an answer. "Kitty, Captain wants to know where you heard the word evidence."

"Meow, I told you, Momma. Meow, the men on the boats said they were getting rid of something called evidence."

"Captain, Kitty insists the men on the boats were getting rid of something they called evidence."

"Well, Sara, it is exciting that Kitty understood a word or two from strangers." Kitty seems agitated and impatient.

"You are such a smart boy for understanding, Kitty, but calm down. Those men could have been talking about good evidence or many other things. They are probably not human varmints at all."

"No!" Kitty yells, sounding just like Captain when he says it.

Captain's eyes get very round, and he looks at Sara with a big grin. "Sara, did Kitty just... did you hear him... Sara, did Kitty just yell the word No?"

Kitty realizes Captain understands. "No, no, no!" he repeats. Kitty jumps into Captain's lap, looking him straight in the eyes.

Captain and Sara look at each other in shock. Their faces beam with pride. Momma had always hoped this moment would come.

"I knew you were going to be as special and talented as your mother! I am so proud of you, Kitty," Captain rewards Kitty with extra hugs and pets.

He continues, "Kitty, for now, let us keep this a secret. Do not talk to any humans, just to Momma and me, OK? Do you understand?"

Momma Sara beams with pride as she explains Captain's concern to Kitty. She wants to ensure that Kitty understands the importance of keeping their unusual gift a secret.

"Yes. Yes!" Captain says. He affectionately pets Kitty.

"No, No!" Kitty repeats again.

"Well, I hope he learns another word soon." They both laugh in delight. Kitty joins in the laughter, although he is not completely sure why they are all laughing.

"Momma, we do have human varmints," Kitty tells Momma. "And I am going to catch them!"

Sara and Captain both begin to consider Kitty's story. "Captain, Kitty really believes he has witnessed something important. Maybe we better keep an open eye, just in case."

Captain quickly responds. "I was just thinking the same thing, Sara."

Browns Lane opens to a picturesque, well-kept, and inviting
home sitting off to the left... Straight ahead, a wide cove,
Browns Bay, looks out into the Severn River.

The weather is perfect. Captain has the truck windows rolled down. The sun is shining, the wind is gently blowing, and there is no chill in the air. He takes his time driving to town.

For a little while, Kitty forgets his adventure to find human varmints and the mysterious skiff boat. For now, his face grins from ear to ear. He stands on his hind legs to allow the wind to blow through his fur.

The wind reminds Kitty of being at sea on Betty. He dreams her billowing sails are pushing them along the coasts of the Gulf of Mexico, around the Keys of Florida and up the east coast in the Atlantic Ocean.

"Betty is faster than the truck, Momma. But this is fun, too."

They reach town and Captain parks the truck in the shade next to the post office. "I am going in for just a few minutes. Stay in the truck, you two. Do not jump out of the window this time. I mean it, Kitty. The last time you followed me into the post office, I did not get out of there for an hour."

Momma nods her head yes. "Kitty, I had to get out of the truck and nap under a tree for you to finish meeting everyone."

"But Momma, I had never been so close to so many people. They were all walking over to me and saying hello. So many people wanted to pet me, Momma. That was a lot of nice people to be polite to."

Kitty stops. He tilts his head back and forth and remembers the men from the night before. *Those mean people are human varmints,* he thinks to himself.

He stands erect and guards the truck while looking for varmints. He studies everyone that comes in and out of the post office that walks through the parking lot, and that goes in and out of nearby stores.

"I do not see any of those human varmints here. When are we going upriver, Momma? I must find that skiff!" Kitty begins to pace back and forth, still on guard.

What Kitty does not notice is the traffic on Main Street. He pays no attention to the passing black truck as it parks in front of the hardware store. Kitty does not see that the driver is a tall man wearing a black hat. Nor does Kitty notice the passenger getting out of the truck has a long, full beard.

"Be patient, Kitty. We will head upriver soon enough."

Finally, Captain comes out of the post office with the mail and a small package.

"Postmaster Annie says to tell you both hello! She also asks us to deliver this package to Miss Brown, seeing we are going upriver anyway. OK, let us head to Browns Bay."

Kitty gets excited to know he is finally heading upriver. "Meow, I just need to get to that skiff, Captain. Please drop me off near the river past the Field of Butterflies. I have to find those varmints, meow!'

Momma interprets Kitty's request to Captain and adds, "I do not like the idea."

Captain chuckles and agrees. "I am not dropping you off, Kitty. You will go with us to pick up the eggs and mending. We will look for varmints along the way."

Kitty pouts as Captain turns off the highway onto Magnolia Road. He sulks aloud, "Meow, at least we are heading upriver, meow."

The drive home is as pleasant as the ride to town. Most of the homes they pass have front porches and dirt driveways. Spattered onto spacious front yards are the falling leaves from many trees, including weeping willows, dogwood trees, and the mighty oak. Magnolias and cedar trees, winter's colorful evergreens, stand out as bright accents. It is indeed a most satisfying drive.

After several miles, Captain enters the boundaries of their estate appropriately named Magnolia Grove. Lined on the right side of Magnolia Road is a row of larger magnolia trees and then a row of tall cedar trees. Behind those, lay plowed fields, and behind that, more forest edged with magnolias. Local farmers plant and harvest the fields on the estate. The many resident animals are safe inhabiting Captain's forests.

On the left side of the road, Magnolia Grove continues with more than two miles of shoreline. It holds several coves and a large, wooded peninsula that points to the mouth of the Mobjack Bay.

From the road, all one can see is a deep forest of majestic trees. However, tucked deep into the forest close to the river, Magnolia Grove Estate protects two hidden homes, Magnolia Grove and Magnolia Cottage.

Captain slows down the truck to admire the beauty of the draping trees lining the road. He sighs in great satisfaction. Captain is very proud of Magnolia Grove Estate.

They pass by the driveway to Magnolia Grove. The gate to the driveway is open, as it is most of the time. Each side of the road's entrance has a red brick column adorned with large stone Bald Eagles.

Next, Captain passes the lane that leads to Magnolia Cottage and its Boat Barn, the Old Dock, and the Field of Butterflies. This is where Grace, Rod, Billy, and Bear now live. Each side of its lane entrance has a smaller version of the same red brick columns adorned with smaller Bald Eagles.

Captain says the Eagles are Gate Guardians that protect Magnolia Grove.

Kitty begins to dream again. The Bald Eagle sculptures remind him of being aboard Betty in the Florida Everglades. That is where he first saw eagles. Along the Everglades, Bald Eagles would hunt and swoop low over Betty and the land. Momma taught Kitty to be very careful around all predatory birds, like eagles.

However, it all can be a little bit confusing. Momma says owls and eagles are dangerous for small animals. Yet, Captain also says that owls stand for wisdom and eagles stand for freedom. Captain says it is wise to fight for freedom.

I need to think more about this. Mrs. Owl is a very wise bird; so, I better ask her.

Kitty's attention goes back to his investigation as the truck passes more forest. Kitty gets worried. "I think we have gone too far, Momma. We may have passed that skiff and cove I need to find."

"We will see." Momma replies, only half paying attention.

Captain announces, "We are on Magnolia Grove until we turn left. Browns Lane separates Magnolia Grove and the Browns Bay Estate. Here is our left turn now."

Kitty looks at Momma with large round eyes. "Meow, I did not know that Captain's land is so big, Momma."

"You understand what Captain is saying, Kitty?"

"Sometimes I do, Momma."

The truck turns left onto Browns Lane. On the right of the smooth sandy lane, a flock of blackbirds feed in a freshly plowed farm field. To the left of the lane lies a thick and intimidating forest. Soon, they see a tiny lane going straight into the woods, but Browns Lane curves left and then right to continue into the forest.

The lane is long and serene. Above it, is a meticulously carved canopy of trees emitting morning sunbeams of filtering light. Birds flitter from branch to branch and announce the arrival of Captain's truck.

"I like little birds, Momma," Kitty says as his eyes delightfully dance over the birds flittering through the trees.

Browns Lane suddenly opens to a picturesque, well-kept, and inviting home sitting off to the left. Old magnolias, weeping willows, and other grand trees shelter the scene in great numbers. Straight ahead, a wide cove looks out into the Severn River.

"There is Browns Bay," says Captain.

Kitty observes that the left bank of Browns Bay is visible all the way to its mouth. However, the right half of the bay hides from view behind a forest of trees.

"Maybe you can find your varmints here, Kitty," Captain laughs.

"Yes, meow." Kitty notes that there are no skiffs in sight. "Meow, varmints, I need to find those human varmints!"

A woman runs out of the house. Kitty growls in surprise when the door slams shut behind her. "Growl… growl…is there a varmint in there, meow?" Kitty scowls.

"Stop this minute. That is rude!" Momma scolds.

Kitty frowns and ducks behind Momma.

The woman continues to the truck. Her dark brown hair sits in a bun on her head, and her face wears a big smile.

Captain gets a big grin on his face, too. "Hello, Hope. How is everything?"

"Hello, Sam! Everything is fine. My brother, Ronnie, is here, you know. Please come in. The mending and eggs are on the table. Three dozen eggs may get her through the weekend with her baking and you men home eating."

Hope sees Kitty. "Why, Sam, who is that with Sara?" Kitty hides behind his Momma.

Momma says I am a handsome young man. Miss Brown is handsome, too, Kitty thinks to himself.

"Hope, this is Sara's son, Kitty. Kitty, this is Miss Brown, our closest neighbor. Hope, may they get out of the truck and stretch? I bet they already smell your kitchen."

Miss Brown's big smile somehow gets larger. "Sam, you always talk to Sara like she is human."

She plays along and talks to Kitty and Sara. "Well, OK. Welcome Kitty, and hello Sara. Kitty, I have a cat door, so you two can come and go as you wish. Our cat, Riley, went with our younger brother, Ramy. Ramy lives in Yorktown. He will be back in a few days. I have treats!"

"Meow. Well, seeing Riley is not here…"

"Sara!" Captain scolds in a loud whisper.

Of course, Miss Brown has no idea Sara understands her. Kitty only understands her big smile, but he does recognize the word, treats.

"Meow, I know the way. Come on, Kitty." Momma jumps out of the truck and goes through the cat door into the house. Kitty follows, thinking and looking about for varmints the entire way.

Entering the kitchen, Kitty sees two doors leading through the house. Kitty darts through one door and quickly runs throughout the house looking for evidence and human varmints. All the doors in the house are open, and all rooms test varmint free.

Kitty enters the kitchen through the other door and reports to Momma, "No varmints here."

"Well, of course there are no varmints here, Kitty. This home belongs to Miss Hope Brown. She and Captain have been good friends a long time."

Hope and Captain enter the kitchen. She offers Captain Sam some iced tea and mother and son some cool water and treats. Kitty realizes Miss Brown is not a human varmint at all, but instead, she is warm and inviting.

Momma is pleased to see Kitty relax. "Kitty, do not go very far from Miss Brown's house. I am going to take a short nap. Captain and Miss Hope always talk for at least an hour."

"Oh, I almost forgot." Captain Sam hands Hope the package he is holding. "Postmaster Annie asked me to deliver this to you."

"Another package delivered this week? Ah, this one is also for one of the men that works for my brother. We can take it down to their campsite in a bit. It is just beyond the dock."

"Meow, dock, you say?" Kitty perks up. "You have a dock, meow?"

Hope starts talking about her brother and the work he is doing on her boathouse and pier. Captain talks about his need of a new roof on the Boat Barn and the upcoming Annual Shoreline Cleanup Day.

With Momma sleeping, and Captain and Miss Brown talking, Kitty slips out of the kitty door and into the yard. The lane they drove in on thins and continues towards Browns Bay. *Where is that pier and boathouse they are talking about?*

Kitty sprints to the cove and ducks behind a holly bush. He looks back towards the house. All is still.

His eyes search the shoreline. Many trees cover the left eastern bank all the way to the mouth of the cove. *That is a lot of forest,* notes Kitty.

Towards the right, the west, Browns Lane turns and continues. The lane is very narrow along the shore, and it has a thick patch of green growing down the middle.

It is a little grass road in the middle of a bigger road! Kitty giggles as he steps into the center. His paws seep low into the thick green carpet. *Oh, my feet feel good. Meow, this is the best grass ever!*

Kitty plays along enjoying the soft green path. Soon he sees the roof of a building. Then he sees its walls, an attached pier, and the water. "Meow, that must be Miss Brown's boathouse."

Hearing no human noises and seeing no people anywhere in sight, Kitty runs towards the boathouse. There are two other boats docked along the pier. *Neither one of those boats were at the Point last night.*

He jumps onto Brown's pier. *Someone sure has done a good job repairing this pier. It looks all new.*

Kitty enters an open door to the boathouse. *This boathouse is almost as big as our Boat Barn,* Kitty observes.

Inside the boathouse, there is a walkway around three sides with workbenches and shelves on the walls. Having no wall, the fourth side opens to the river. *Boats can easily come in here to dock.* On the workbenches and shelves, there are boxes of nails, tools, and supplies. On the deck is a pile of boards for repairs. "Nothing looks strange here." Kitty meows.

Kitty looks down at the boathouse's floor of water. He feels his heart drop to the bottom of his stomach, and he almost loses his breath. In the water, towards the front of the boathouse, docks a long grey skiff.

He cautiously looks around and very carefully approaches the skiff to get a better look. "There is that varmint skiff!" Kitty shrieks. "So, this is where it lives!"

The tide is high, and Kitty has no problem jumping into the skiff. He sniffs and looks around. *Yes, those human varmints used this very same skiff last night. I need to find some evidence. What is this skiff hiding?*

The skiff is clean now, but it still has that funny smell. It smells, uh, maybe, a little like plastic. Kitty searches the entire boat but does not find anything that appears suspicious.

He jumps out of the skiff and back into the boathouse. Looking up onto the wall he had entered through, Kitty sees shelves filled with cans and jars. *There could be evidence over there. That is a lot of stuff.* He jumps up on the shelves and starts sniffing. *I wonder what is in those cans. Is it evidence?*

Kitty continues sniffing and roaming in and out of the containers on the shelves. He brushes too close to a can and knocks it over. The can rolls into a plastic jar, and then the jar falls and rolls. They both roll and knock into other containers. Cans and plastic jars start rolling and crashing onto the shelf below and onto the walkway deck. *Good thing there is a board to stop that stuff from rolling into the water.* "That would be very bad, meow."

Oh yes, this is just like what I did in Captain's Boat Barn. And he was somewhat mad. "I better get out of here, meow." Kitty looks out from the Brown's boathouse and does not see any sign of people.

In a small clearing close to the boathouse, Kitty sees a large van with a padlock on the back doors. *That must be where all the tools are. There may be evidence in there.*

In front of the van, a small brown pickup truck and a long motorhome sit. Kitty starts sniffing around for clues that may lead him to more evidence. *Now, where is that varmint with the black hat? He must be somewhere close to his skiff.*

Kitty's keen ears hear someone approaching. He decides to hide and ducks behind the truck.

Peeking from behind a tire, Kitty sees Captain and Miss Brown walking towards the motorhome. Miss Brown is carrying the postal package Captain delivered.

"Let me give this package to my brother, and I will show you the progress on the pier and boathouse." Miss Brown knocks on the door. "Ronnie!" She sweetly yells.

Miss Brown has a sparkle in her voice. *Her voice sounds like a big smile.* Kitty thinks and gets confused. *Meow, why is there a varmint skiff here in nice Miss Brown's boathouse? She needs protection! I must figure out what is going on here!*

The door opens to the motorhome. A tall and muscular man exits the motorhome. His smile is almost as large as Miss Brown's smile.

"Hey, Hope. It is a most pleasant day! The boys and I are waiting for a delivery of materials to start your roof this afternoon or tomorrow, probably after fishing, of course!"

"Hi, Ronnie, I would like you to meet Captain Sam. He owns Magnolia Grove next door."

"Well, nice to meet you, Captain! You have a beautiful place next door. We enjoy it from the river. Would you two come in for some coffee? We can watch life on the cove for a bit."

Kitty observes from behind the truck tire. His mind is figuring out things as hard as it possibly can.

That Ronnie person sure is not acting like a human varmint, either. He certainly is not one of the four men from last night. What is going on around here?

"No thanks, Ronnie," Hope Brown tells her brother. "I am going to show Sam the boathouse and the pier's progress. Then I must get back to my sewing. School fall dances and early Holiday orders are demanding my time."

Captain acknowledges her hard work. "Hope, remember how many dresses you altered last year? Wasn't it around fifteen?"

"Actually, I managed eighteen alterations. I already have twenty-nine gowns and suits for this year. Business is picking up!"

"Ronnie," Captain continues, "since you are working here at your sister's place already, I was wondering if you would be interested in giving me a bid on replacing the roof on my dry dock Boat Barn."

Ronnie gets a big smile and replies, "The boys and I would be pleased to extend our fishing time here in Virginia. I am at your service, Captain. Shall I come by tomorrow after lunch, say, about one? I can give you a price to see if it fits your budget. My plan is to work on Hope's boathouse the rest of the day."

"That is good timing, Ronnie. Before you arrive, I will have a little time to recuperate from being stuffed by one of my sister's grand lunches."

Miss Brown interrupts. "I almost forgot. I brought another package for you, Ronnie. It is the same as the others, addressed to Mervin and in care of Ronnie Brown here at Browns Bay."

Ronnie laughs. "The last overnight package was beef jerky from Mervin's wife. I told him we are not so back country that we cannot get to a store!"

"That figures," his sister giggles and replies. "Well, I will see you for dinner at 6:00 sharp!"

Ronnie smiles and hugs his sister. "We may go out on the Mobjack to go fishing a few hours tonight, too." They all say farewell, and Captain and Miss Brown walk over to the pier and boathouse.

Hope shows Sam her brother's handsome 27' Judge Eastern. Captain admires the well-kept fishing boat.

Then he looks over the pier's new boards. "Your brother and his workers have done good work here, Hope. What are they repairing on the boathouse?"

"I am getting a new roof and many old boards replaced. They are beginning to crack and break."

"That certainly sounds similar to what I need over at the Boat Barn."

Entering the boathouse, Captain and Hope see cans and jars everywhere. Hope shrieks in surprise, "What in the world happened here?"

Captain mutters to himself, "It can't be possible, but it sure looks like Kitty."

"Let me help you clean this up, Hope."

Captain and Miss Brown seem not to notice the grey skiff in the water nor the odd smell emitting from it.

Kitty watches the motorhome and the boathouse. *Captain has found the mess in the boathouse by now. He will know I did it. Oh, why am I so clumsy and messy? Captain says I am mischievous.*

Kitty knows he has run out of time for investigating this area today. He cuts behind the van and runs back to the lane and its center row of soft green grass.

The motorhome door opens and Ronnie Brown steps out and onto the ground. Looking around, he smiles as he spots a young calico cat running away from the camping spot.

Ronnie pulls a phone out of his pocket and dials a number. Someone answers, and Ronnie tells the person on the other end, "Good fortune may be ours Mr. Green. I have found a new cover that will allow us to stay here longer. I just need to make sure we get a repair contract on the Boat Barn next door."

Ronnie listens. "Yes, next door. Captain Sam needs his Boat Barn repaired."

Ronnie listens again. "Yes, I said Captain Sam. Can't you hear me?"

When Kitty reaches the left curve that heads towards Miss Brown's house, he stops and looks towards Browns Bay. Kitty again notices the heavily wooded shore. Looking closer, he begins to make out an almost hidden path running between the edge of the trees and the water's edge.

Without thinking, Kitty takes off down the path. He follows the shoreline all the way to the mouth of the cove before he stops. The path makes a sharp turn left and continues along the river as far as Kitty can see. *Wow. I wonder how far that path goes.*

Kitty suddenly remembers Captain and Momma. *Oh no, I had better hurry! They will be looking for me.* Kitty runs back along the path as fast as he can and into Miss Brown's open yard.

Kitty is relieved Captain and Miss Brown are still walking towards Miss Brown's house. Kitty passes them unnoticed and jumps through the cat door and into the kitchen.

The noise wakens Momma.

"Momma, Momma, I found the varmint skiff! I found it!"

"What, Kitty, you found a skiff?" Momma asks him.

"Yes, the long varmint skiff from last night is in Miss Brown's boathouse!"

"Kitty, there are many skiffs. Captain even has a long skiff. It docks close to the shore."

"I am telling you, Momma. It is the same one! It smells funny!"

"You better make sure before jumping to any conclusions, young man. We need to hear what Captain has to say."

Miss Brown and Captain enter her kitchen. She gives Captain three dozen eggs and a neatly tied bundle of repaired jeans. "I want you all to come back soon. Kitty, next time you and your mother can go down by the cove to play. Sara knows the way."

Momma translates and Kitty answers with a smile. "Meow, yes ma'am, we will, meow."

"Isn't he cute?" Miss Brown laughs. "Kitty sounds like he is answering me."

Miss Brown waves goodbye, and the three of them drive back through the tree-canopied lane. Momma explains to Captain that Kitty believes he has found the skiff from the night before.

"Do not forget to tell him I could not find the tall man in the black hat. That is important, Momma. He must be somewhere around here. I must find that man and investigate him."

Momma sighs and explains to Captain about the missing tall man with the black hat. "Kitty insists that man is close and important to the case."

Captain thinks things over and replies. "So, Kitty did not see any of the varmints from last night. You know almost everyone along the river has a skiff, Sara. I do not know what to think. We will keep an eye on things and see what happens. Just in case, we better keep a lookout for those varmints."

Kitty has forgotten to pay attention. He is thinking about his morning adventure. He knows that Browns Bay is the same cove the varmint skiff entered last night. He also knows he has found the same skiff in Miss Brown's boathouse. With certainty, Kitty decides Miss Brown and her brother are not human varmints.

Why did that skiff come across the river and meet a trawler in the dark of night? Why did it secretly transport evidence while hiding in front of the Point? Most importantly, why did it dock in Browns Bay? I need to go back there and investigate.

Kitty thinks about returning to Browns Bay. *Browns Lane is long enough, but the big, paved road to get to Browns Lane is much longer. Momma will ground me for a long time if she catches me walking on any big, paved road.*

Kitty tilts his head back and forth and thinks. *Captain says Browns Lane separates Browns Bay from Magnolia Grove. That path I found at Browns Bay turns towards Magnolia Grove. Maybe, yes, maybe it connects to the Field of Butterflies and the Old Dock!*

Aloud Kitty yells, "Well, meow, maybe it does!"

Kitty gets excited. "Meow, I need to get to the Old Dock!"

It has been such a busy morning, and Kitty begins to get tired. He dreams of reaching Browns Bay from the Field of Butterflies as the truck hums him to sleep.

Captain departs Browns Bay Estate and heads towards home. In the rear-view mirror, Captain sees a black truck also turn from Browns Lane onto Magnolia Road. It quickly drives up behind Captain's truck, appears very impatient, and speeds past.

"That driver sure is in a hurry, Sara. I cannot say I know that black truck. It may be one of Ronnie's workers. Come to think of it, I did not see that truck at their camp site."

Captain notices the man driving wearing a black hat. His head almost touches the roof of his truck. Captain sees he also has a passenger with a long, full beard.

"I do not know those two men either." Captain's tone expresses interest.

"Captain," Sara has a questioning look on her face, "do you think…"

Captain interrupts. "Sara! No, those men cannot be the same…do you think that Kitty somehow… Sara, exactly where did Kitty say that skiff went?"

4 ~ THE PATH

"You are seeing things or just crazy. Everybody knows cats and
squirrels do not hang out together."

C aptain's truck sits under a shade tree in front of his home at Magnolia Grove. With the windows rolled down, a breeze blows through the truck and creates a pleasant atmosphere for Kitty to sleep. The morning adventures at Browns Bay have been tiring, and he has worked himself to the need of a noontime nap.

Kitty wakes up and stretches. He arches his back and stretches again. His stomach begins to growl and churn. Kitty leaps out of the window of the shaded truck and races to the kitchen.

He starts remembering his morning adventure up until now. *I sure am glad Captain let me sleep. I might have a long night tonight investigating.*

Kitty bounces into the kitchen.

"Well, there you are, Kitty. Did you have a nice, long nap?" Captain sits working in his office that is located beside the kitchen.

"Meow, yes!" Kitty starts chomping on lunch, and, as usual, food scatters two feet out in all directions.

"Don't you think it is time for you to be a bit more careful and try to be tidy, Kitty?" Captain looks at the food all over the kitchen floor. "Your mother and Grace spoil you. You need to start cleaning up after yourself young man."

"Mm," Kitty thinks. *Captain seems serious about the food I leave on the floor. He does not understand. Miss Grace sings while she cleans up my food. Then she throws the pieces out for the little birds. I make her very happy!*

Captain tries to tell Kitty, "Talk to Momma after lunch! She has something to discuss with you, adventurous one."

After lunch, Kitty checks in with Momma. "I am going down to the Old Dock to find MadmanMax, Momma. Maybe he knows more about that skiff."

"You are always talking about that squirrel. Why have I not met this MadmanMax, Kitty? What an odd name."

"Well, Momma, cats and dogs are dangerous for squirrels. We have both here on Magnolia Grove. MadmanMax says that squirrels have to be stinking careful around here."

Momma responds, "Well, that explains nothing, Kitty. You are a cat.

Oh, go, have fun, and be careful." She adds, "I want you home in time for dinner. And Kitty, you better not miss your lessons or walking Billy to the bus stop tomorrow morning, Son."

Kitty knows Momma is serious with the word, "Son."

"I will, and I won't, Momma!" Kitty laughs as he begins to run out the door. He really does love his morning lessons with Momma. *But I have been so busy!*

"Oh Kitty, stop! Captain wants me to discuss something important with you."

Kitty stops and turns around. "He does, Momma? He has something important to discuss with me, Momma?"

"Yes, Kitty, Captain wants to know everything you find out during your investigations."

In excitement, Kitty dances, turning round and round with happiness. "So, Captain believes me? Did he tell you so, Momma?"

Momma explains. "Yes, Kitty, of course Captain believes you.

This morning, as we were leaving the Brown Estate, Captain saw a black truck pull out of Browns Lane and come up behind our truck. A very tall man with a black hat was driving, and his passenger had a long, full beard."

Kitty stands tall and pays attention. "I told you, Momma! I did tell you both! You must tell me, Momma! Tell me everything!"

"There is not much more to tell you, Kitty. The black truck was in a great hurry this morning and sped past us on the road. Captain does not know the black truck or the two men that were inside it. He thinks that maybe the men work for Ronne Brown. They might be camped somewhere on the Brown Estate."

"I hope not, Momma. Miss Brown and her brother, Mr. Brown, seem to be very nice people. They do not act like varmints."

Momma continues, "Captain is wondering where the black truck was during our visit to the Brown Estate this morning. He did not see the truck at Miss Brown's house, nor did he see it down by Ronnie Brown's campsite near her boathouse. Still, the black truck came out of Browns Lane behind us. It had to be on the estate."

"That is very mysterious, Momma. So where was that black truck hiding anyway?"

I will find that black truck's hiding spot!

Momma suddenly realizes Kitty just mentioned Ronnie Brown. "Kitty, how did you meet Miss Brown's brother, Ronnie Brown?"

"I did not meet him, Momma. I just saw him at the campsite. He was talking to Captain and Miss Brown. And there was no black truck there either Momma. I was investigating good! And that is when I found that varmint skiff, too, Momma."

"I see. I hope you are very careful, Kitty. Captain is not overly concerned, yet he does want to know everything that goes on. Do you understand, Kitty?"

"OK, Momma. I understand. I must go now. MadmanMax will help me, Momma. He and Mr. and Mrs. Owl might know what to do."

This time, Momma's eyes get huge. "Owls, Kitty? What owls might know what to do?"

"Mr. and Mrs. Owl live on the Point, Momma. I work for them."

"I think you better explain, Kitty." Just what do you do on the Point for owls?" Momma is being very careful. She fears that owl family that lives on the Point is tricking her son. She wonders if Kitty remembers that these birds eat small animals.

"You do not understand, Momma. I report to them where all the fattest and tastiest mice are living. Then the Owls let me explore the Point, Momma. It is so much fun to play there, Momma!"

"Oh my, Kitty, I am not sure about any of this. That Owl family is very dangerous to many animals.

It is true that people like owls very much. Owls are known to be very, very wise birds. They also pay attention to everything that goes on around them.

However, Kitty, your Mr. and Mrs. Owl also like to hunt small prey. You will stay away from the Owls until I meet them."

"But, Momma, the Owls and I both eat mice. I just let Mr. and Mrs. Owl have the best mice on the Point. They need me to find them, Momma."

Momma gets stern. "Kitty, I mean what I say. You are not to go back to that Point until I meet the Owls. Whether you like it or not, you are still young; I need to know you are playing in a safe place."

Kitty lowers his eyebrows and pouts. "Captain says the Point is a safe place for me to play, Momma. You heard him. He says that…"

Sara cuts Kitty off in mid-sentence. "Captain is not aware of the new development and danger. The current situation with the Owls is very serious, Kitty. I had better not have tell you again."

Kitty knows when to give up. "OK, Momma, but you will see. Mr. and Mrs. Owl like me."

Kitty turns around and mutters to himself, "I think."

"Anyway, Momma, I am going the other way to the Old Dock. I must see MadmanMax. I will be back in time for dinner!"

Kitty walks away shaking his head and thinking. *Momma sure does not understand my job. I am very important around here. I must protect Magnolia Grove! And I must help everyone around here that needs me!*

Kitty heads across the front yard and through the trees to Grace's house. He forgets his mission for a few seconds and almost goes inside for a snack of sardines he can smell. *Those sardines must wait. I have my investigating to do. But I must be home for dinner, when the sun hits the top of the trees.*

As Kitty runs past the Boat Barn, he remembers the first time he explored inside the huge building.

It is such a fun place to play, Kitty thinks. *It is so full of fun smells, boat equipment, and tools. It has so many places to hide. There are also many tasty mice running around that I do not have to tell the Owls about!*

However, during that first visit, Kitty accidentally knocked over a can of paint, and it went everywhere. That made Kitty so jittery that when he ran out of the barn, he knocked over an entire shelf of nails and screws.

I knocked over all that stuff in Miss Brown's boathouse, too. Maybe I am too clumsy. Captain always says I am too inquisitive. I find adventures!

Forgetting his lesson just learned, Kitty reaches the Old Dock and the Virginia pine tree his friend calls home.

MadmanMax is busy digging holes in the ground to bury his winter nuts. He looks up at the panting cat.

"What do you know, Kid? Make it fast. I am very busy here as you can see. Winter is coming. No time to spare."

Kitty tries to oblige the squirrel and speaks very quickly. "MadmanMax, MadmanMax, am I glad to see you! We got varmints, bad human varmints at Miss Brown's place. I need to get to Browns Bay where that skiff is. That varmint in the black hat is up to no good, too. They are moving evidence, MadmanMax, evidence! And they are here on our river!"

MadmanMax stops still and stands up on his hind legs to study a very serious Kitty. The generally bad-tempered squirrel takes on a concerned look. "OK, Kid, you have my attention. Are you in trouble again?"

"I do not think so, MadmanMax. I think we all might be in danger."

MadmanMax sits down. "You better slow down. Start from the beginning. Take your time and tell me your story, Kid."

Kitty sits. He again explains the story and tells MadmanMax about seeing the flare the night before. He explains how the men on the fishing trawler and skiff met to move crates from one boat to another.

"What is in the crates, Kid?"

"I do not know, MadmanMax, but those men definitely acted suspicious!"

Kitty leans closer to his friend. "They are hiding everything in secret. They tried to be very quiet. Then they dropped that crate, and they acted so afraid, MadmanMax. They thought something horrible was going to happen!

That skiff loaded heavy with crates came from that hidden cove across the river. The trawler took the crates and went back into the Mobjack Bay."

"Kid, and after all that, where are you saying that stinking skiff went?"

"The tall man with the black hat took it upriver to Miss Brown's boathouse, MadmanMax. I found it there this morning! It may be there right now!"

"OK, Kid, so what's the plan?"

"I have not figured it all out yet, MadmanMax. I found a path heading west from Browns Bay. Can you help me look for it from the Field of Butterflies?" Kitty implores.

"I don't have to find it. I live here, Kid. I hunt that path for food almost every day."

"You do? Please, please, can we go now? I must be home by the time the sun hits the top of the trees for dinner or Momma is going to ground me."

The squirrel gives in. "Well, I can tell you are not going to stop talking until I take you to that path. Follow me."

They cross the Field of Butterflies to the edge of the woods where Kitty frequently hunts mice. MadmanMax leads them very close to the river and then scurries around the first thick bush on the waters' edge. He turns around to Kitty, who is close to his bushy tail.

Kitty gets very excited, and his eyes widen to the size of saucers. "How did I miss this path? Have you been to the end? Does it end at the next cove?"

"I don't know, Kid. I see many boats going in and out of that cove west of Magnolia Grove, but I have never been over there. My territory ends up the path apiece. I will show you."

They travel up the path for many acres, and then the squirrel stops. "This is the end of my territory, Kid."

Kitty starts running farther up the path. "Come on, MadmanMax, let's go find the cove!"

"Well, Kid. Squirrels are a bit territorial. We may have to negotiate passage. The neighboring squirrels do not like strangers wandering about their turf."

Kitty stands tall with no fear. "Well, MadmanMax, we will tell them this is my Captain's land called Magnolia Grove. We will tell them that he happens to own the territory all the way to Browns Bay. Those squirrels will let us pass."

"If you say so, Kid. But squirrels can be as bad as a coyote when they hang in a gang."

The odd-looking duo work their way along the path. They take breaks for MadmanMax to collect nuts. He piles them along the side of the path to gather later.

Every now and then, MadmanMax dashes up a tree to see how they are progressing. This time, he reports that he sees a cove in the distance.

"We are almost there," Kitty yells in glee. "Let us go! Hurry down, Max!"

Suddenly, a grey squirrel gang appears. Looking mean and dangerous, they jump in the middle of the path, stopping Kitty and MadmanMax from traveling along the path any farther.

A large squirrel steps forward, asserting himself as leader. He laughs in a deep gruff voice and demands, "What are you doing here?" The other squirrels behind him start snickering.

Kitty keeps his senses and starts laughing too.

The leader growls, "What are you laughing about, Cat?"

"Your laughing made me laugh." Kitty casually answers.

One of the snickering squirrels asks, "Hey cat, don't you know when to be afraid?"

The second snickering squirrel looks at MadmanMax and asks, "What are you doing outside your territory, and why are you traveling with this enemy cat?"

"Traveling," answers MadmanMax.

"We are not afraid of you," Kitty interrupts. "We need passage back and forth through your territory to the next cove, and you will give it to us because this land is owned by my Captain."

"Well, la-de-da, and your Captain ain't here. Anyway, he cannot find us back here in the woods. Why should we care about your Captain?"

The leader takes another step closer. Kitty is still and holds his ground.

The leader speaks back to his gang. "Let's tear the cat's fur out, break his leg, and throw him in the river."

MadmanMax steps forward. "In that case, you all will have to fight both of us. The locals call me MadmanMax for very good reason, boys." He stands beside Kitty tall, strong, and as a force to fear. "I am sure you have heard of me."

Indeed, they have heard much about MadmanMax. He is known as the fiercest squirrel in Magnolia Grove.

MadmanMax whispers to Kitty, "If anything happens, run to the river. You can swim. They prefer not to swim and soon will give up on you. The tide is going east, and it will help carry you towards your house. You will soon be able to swim to shore and home."

"OK, MadmanMax, I will. But, what about you?"

Kitty tilts his head back and forth and thinks further about their situation. Suddenly, he smiles and turns to his companion and loudly says, "You know, MadmanMax, I am not in the mood for a fight today. Why fight to gain passage?"

The leader takes the bait and asks, "And just how do you think you are getting past us without a fight, Cat?"

All the other squirrels start repeating the leader's question. "Get past us without a fight? How are you going to get past us without a fight?"

Kitty keeps calm and completely ignores the repeated question. By this time, the riled squirrels are jumping up and down.

Kitty continues, "MadmanMax, let us do this the easy way. I am sure Mr. and Mrs. Owl, will help us rid of these pests that are squatting on Captain's land. We will go back to the Point and tell them all about our problem."

Kitty and MadmanMax slowly start walking back towards home. Kitty whispers, "Watch this MadmanMax. They do not want to be on the Mr. and Mrs. Owl's Most Wanted List."

"Me neither," replies MadmanMax as he calmly keeps walking. "I hope you know what you are doing, Kid."

"Me too," mutters Kitty under his breath.

The leader of the varmint squirrel gang is the first to speak. "Wait, Cat. Did you say Mr. and Mrs. Owl are your friends?"

Kitty turns around and casually announces, "If you please, my friends are Mr. and Mrs. Great Horned Owl."

The squirrels take a step back and start whispering to each other.

Kitty further explains, "I have full passage on their territory, and they have hunting rights to all of Captain's land. I do intend to introduce you squirrels to Mr. and Mrs. Owl." Kitty and MadmanMax slowly start walking towards home again.

"Be ready to run, Kid," MadmanMax whispers.

"Wait a minute, Cat." The leader scratches his ear. "Uh, all of us need not be so hasty."

Kitty and MadmanMax slowly turn around and cautiously listen for the upcoming proposition.

The leading squirrel comes up with the anticipated plan. "Uh, I tell you what. If you do not tell the, uh, Owls about us, we will give you passage across our territory for the cost of fifty nuts per trip."

"50 nuts?" Kitty laughs. They start walking towards home again.

The squirrel gang chatters among themselves.

The leader speaks again. "Uh, OK, well, uh, with no strings attached. But the Owls won't eat us... deal?"

Kitty sees the leader tremble and hears his voice crack with fear.

"Deal," is all the gang hears from Kitty. He and MadmanMax boldly walk past the cowering squirrels and continue along the path. Neither of them looks back, but MadmanMax keeps his ears alert, knowing there could be an ambush.

"I hate stinking gangs. They give us squirrels a bad name."

MadmanMax runs up a tree and scouts the area. He runs back down and announces quietly, "All is clear!"

MadmanMax looks at Kitty. "That was good, Kid."

"Thanks, MadmanMax. That was the first time I have been afraid since I was alone at the Old Dock, when I met you."

"Well, you didn't show it. You were cool and calm, Kid. You really handled that unruly scurry of squirrels with confidence. You will make a great leader, Kid."

"Gosh, MadmanMax, thanks, that means a lot coming from you."

"I tell you what, Kid. You can call me Max, well, when we are alone. My family and friends call me Max."

"Thanks Max."

"I guess you earned it. You are not such a bad cat."

Max decides this is as good a time as any to ask the big question: "By the way, Kid, how did you know those varmint men were hiding evidence? Who told you what they were saying?"

Kitty starts to blush and shows a bit of panic. He slowly dances around in a few circles and stammers. "Well, Max, you see, well, I just... Oh, Max, I cannot tell!"

Max gazes at Kitty and admires his conviction in keeping his word. "Can you understand people, Kitty?"

Kitty lowers his head and innocently dances around again.

Max laughs. "I knew it! You are just like your momma!"

Kitty gasps in shock. He looks in all directions and whispers, "Max, how did you know? Who told you about Momma?"

Talking low to soothe Kitty, Max tells Kitty his own secret. "Well, Kid, sometime back, I was napping on my back-porch branch minding my own business when Captain and your momma came walking by our tree. Captain was going on and on about something. I sure could not understand him. When he stopped talking, your momma responded in his language. I could not understand her either. Your momma and Captain frequently walk around Magnolia Grove talking to each other, Kitty."

Kitty is amazed at Max's knowledge. "Wow, and you never let the others know the secret?"

"Nah, I respect privacy. It is none of my business. To let you know, Kid, the local animals scatter when Captain and your momma come around. Your secret is safe between us." Max starts digging for treasures.

"Thanks. I appreciate that. Do you also have family and friends? Where do they live? Why have I not met them?"

"Of course, I have family and friends, Kid. The wife does not like you much, so she stays in our treehouse whenever you come around. Our young recently moved out. They each have a few acres close by in the woods, as do the rest of my family and some good friends. This is a big place, Kid, and we control a lot of turf."

Max looks taller and larger as he speaks about his family and friends. "Actually Kid, all the squirrels all stay away from you for pretty much the same reason. They do not like you."

Kitty looks curious. "Why do they not like me, Max? You like me. The animals on the Point like me. Your family and friends do not even know me."

"Well for one thing, Kid, they see you catch those mice at the edge of the woods and eat them. They think you are going to eat them, too. That makes them very leery of you, Kid."

"I will not eat them, Max. You can tell all of them that I will not eat squirrels. I never wanted to eat a squirrel, anyway, all that bushy fur and stuff in my teeth sounds awful. I will leave them alone, Max."

"I will tell them." Max says. "I already know that anyway, Kid. You sure are a different kind of cat."

Max and Kitty finally reach the point located at the mouth of Browns Bay. "I made it this far earlier from Miss Brown's house, Max! There is the boathouse! Can you see Miss Brown's house over there?"

Max yells from a treetop. "I see it, Kid."

They both make their way along the cove and up the lane with the green grass cushion down the middle. "Doesn't this grass feel great, Max?"

"This is not grass, Kid. This is moss. There are many kinds of moss. It grows where there is little sun, like here under the trees and on the north side of other trees and buildings."

"Moss," Kitty repeats as his feet seep into the green carpet. "I like moss."

They both spot the pier and boathouse. There is no sign of anyone. "Where are Ronnie Brown's workers? I want to see if they are the same varmints that were getting rid of the evidence last night."

Kitty takes Max inside the boathouse. He runs to the front to show Max the skiff. "There is that varmint skiff! It is still here, Max."

They both investigate the skiff while Kitty tells Max about his morning investigation. He explains that the reason for the boathouse's current mess is that he had knocked over all the jars and cans.

Max scratches his head. "What mess, Kid? I see no mess."

Kitty looks around. "Hey, Max, someone cleaned up the mess I made already. Someone has been here."

"Yeah, Kid. I am telling you that everything is too clean around here. The only out of place thing is that sickening smell. It is surely nothing to eat or use to make a nest."

"So, you smell it too, Max?"

"I don't know how anyone could miss that stinking smell, Kid."

Kitty then takes Max to the campsite where he previously had found the locked work van, the motorhome, and the small brown pickup truck.

"Captain said a black truck with two of the human varmints in it drove out of here behind us this morning. I was sleeping, so I missed it. Max, I never saw a black truck parked around here either."

"Well, where do you think that path goes, Kid?"

Kitty looks in the direction Max is pointing. The lane with the green moss keeps going past the motorhome.

Kitty cannot wait. He runs ahead of Max. Shortly, he returns and reports. "This lane turns right into the woods and ends towards the plowed field at Browns Lane. We saw the same lane this morning on the way to Miss Brown's house. This must be where the black truck hides."

Kitty looks up at the sky. "The sun is more than halfway between lunch and dinner. Max, we had better head back home. It will take us some time to get there."

As they walk past the campsite and towards the path, Kitty and Max size up their situation. It has taken a long time to get this far, but they realize they have accomplished much today. Kitty thinks ahead, "The next time we come, it won't take so much time to get back to Browns Bay."

"Yeah, not so much stinking time," Max repeats.

Feeling a little bit tired, they meander more slowly on the path along Browns Bay. When they reach the cleared area that turns east towards home, Max stops. "We have enough time not to wear ourselves out, Kid. Take a rest."

"You are just hungry, Max." Kitty laughs and lies on the ground to rest and admire the river. Max eats a few pine nuts out of a ripe pinecone.

As he runs up a pine tree looking for another ripe pinecone, Kitty yells up, "Max, do you think those varmints will come out on the river again tonight?"

"I don't know about tonight, Kid. But I do know I see your skiff coming out on the river right now."

"What? Max, you see the skiff now?" Kitty jumps to the point's edge and leans to the water. Max jumps down to his side.

"Yes, Max, I hear it. That is the same skiff. Here it comes. I see it, now."

Both stay perfectly still as the skiff slowly goes by. Inside the skiff are two of the human varmints Kitty has been looking for. One is the tall man with the black hat and the other is the man with the long, full beard.

"There they are, Max. There are two of the human varmints. The boat sits high in the water, Max; so, it has no load on it now. That man in the black hat sure likes to ride close to the shore. Last night, he touched the Old Dock with his hand as he passed. He did not see me, but he was close."

Inside the skiff, the man with the long, full beard gazes over towards the cleared area at the eastern tip of Browns Bay. He shakes his head and double looks again.

"I just saw a cat and a squirrel together on that sandy point."

"You are seeing things or crazy," states the tall man with the black hat. "Everybody knows cats and squirrels do not hang out together. They are enemies."

The skiff starts to move out into the river. "I bet that varmint skiff is going to the hidden cove across the river, Max. I bet they will pick up more evidence for tonight."

As the two of them push towards home, Kitty and Max watch the skiff slowly cross over the river and disappear out of sight. When they reach the Field of Butterflies and the Old Dock, the sun is close to the top of the trees.

"Thanks Max. This has been a great afternoon. We did good investigating. I had better run home. If I am late for dinner, Momma will ground me. I do not need that trouble now. We have a lot more investigating to do!"

"OK, Kid. I am going to eat and go to bed myself. The wife will have questions that I will have to answer."

Kitty smiles as he looks at his close friend. "You can call me Kitty, Max. Everyone else does."

"I like the name Kid," responds Max.

Kitty laughs. "OK. See you tomorrow! Do not forget to tell all the squirrels I am a protector and friend! Especially tell Mrs. Max!"

"Sure, Kid, I will." Max heads towards home muttering, "Like the Mrs. is going to be interested in a cat protector."

5 ~ A STRANGE ALLIANCE

"Before I tear you to pieces and eat you, stranger, tell me why
you dare come to our Point at night?"

Kitty bounces into the kitchen as Billy and Captain walk into the house. The table is set, and dinner is on the table.

"You are all just in time. Wash your hands." Grace looks pleased to see everyone ready to eat.

Billy leans down to pet Kitty. "I missed you today, Kitty. I had band practice. Captain picked me up."

Momma and Kitty start eating their fish. "Mm, meow, this is good," Momma politely meows between bites.

Kitty gobbles, trying very hard to keep his food in the bowl and inside his mouth. "Meow, thanks, meow, this is good." Kitty stops. He looks at Captain and then Miss Grace, and clearly asks, "What is this?"

Captain's mouth drops open. Sara hears it, Billy misses it, and Grace answers without thinking. "It is rainbow trout, freshwater trout." She reaches down and pets both Kitty and Sara. "I bought a ten-pound supply. It is in the freezer. I knew it would be a favorite." Grace goes into the butler pantry.

Sara and Captain are frozen in place. Grace pays no attention to the fact that she just answered Kitty's question. Captain leans over and whispers to Sara, "Maybe she thinks Billy or I asked the question."

Sara looks a little stressed wondering if Kitty's secret is about to be known to all. She manages a smile. "You did want him to learn a new word, Captain. That was three new words."

It is not long before Captain starts laughing. "Would you look at that boy? Kitty has once again fallen asleep in his food bowl."

Captain is curious about Kitty's investigations. "We will have to wait for his sleuthing report. Today, I bet he found his way back to Browns Bay along the sandy shoreline past the Old Dock."

"Kitty said he was going to get that crazy squirrel, MadmanMax, to help him, Captain."

"Well, at least he was not alone. He sure can pick up some strange friends. Aw, Kitty needs a ride to bed. I will be right back."

Captain picks up Kitty and carries him to his room. Momma follows, and Kitty never stirs.

"That reminds me, Captain, speaking of strange friends, do you know Mr. and Mrs. Owl?"

Wednesday night

The night air feels cool as Sara works her way to the Point Kitty loves so much. The path through the woods is narrow and very low to the ground. "How did Kitty find this?"

Sara cannot help but be afraid. She knows her own eyesight is excellent, but the Owls can hear and see much better than she can. Sara keeps her eyes open for a place to run if the Owls should attack.

She shakes off her fear and talks to herself. "I must talk to that Mr. and Mrs. Owl. What do they want with my son?"

The pathway widens just a bit. In the night sky, Sara sees a huge soaring figure above her. It turns and glides directly towards the path Sara stands. Before she can think long enough to run, a mighty Owl quickly swoops to the ground. It blocks Sara from moving forward.

Sara shakes. In front of her is the largest male owl she has ever seen. She searches each side of the path for potential escape, eyeing some low and thick bushes as possible protection.

Attempting to stand her ground, she looks in the eyes of the Owl and nervously states, "Oh my, you are a big one. I was hoping for a smaller Eastern Screech Owl."

The Great Horned Owl looks at Sara with surprise. He admires her bravery, considering the situation. He turns his huge head around in all directions as if he is looking for someone.

"An Eastern Screech Owl, indeed. That would be a snack for me, like you soon might be." The huge and offended Mr. Owl spreads his wings with indignity and takes a step closer to Sara.

"Before I tear you to pieces and eat you, stranger, tell me why do you dare come to our Point at night? Have you no fear, no sense?"

Sara knows she must keep her composure. Mr. Owl is four times her height, and his wingspread is over four feet wide. He is indeed a most threatening and towering creature.

Suddenly, things get worse, and Sara starts shaking again. An even larger member of the Owl family, a huge female, eloquently lowers herself behind Sara. She has a wingspan of almost five feet.

Sara is about to run with all her might when she hears a soothing foreign voice. "Papa, calm down your feathers. This is Master Kitty's mother, Miss Sara."

"You, you, you know me?" She hopes the Owls do not see how badly she is trembling.

The beautiful and elegant Mrs. Owl smiles at Sara. "Why of course we know you, my dear. Now calm down, calm down. It is important that Papa put on a good show. He must protect me. Everything is fine now."

"Then you are the Mr. and Mrs. Owl Kitty talks about?"

"Yes, we are Mr. and Mrs. Great Horned Owl, at your service. Now tell us why you are here tonight."

Sara begins to relax. "So, are you Kitty's friends?" She sees no reason to beat around the bush.

Mr. Owl speaks out and explains. "Well, uh, let us just say we have an arrangement. He reports where all the delectable mice are, and in turn, we do not kill him. We then let him have passage on our home."

"Yes," Mrs. Owl adds, "We make him earn his way. We cannot have him going around trusting every owl he meets."

"I see," replies Sara. She sits and takes her turn. "I told Kitty he could not come back here until I talk to you. I must say, I certainly am glad to meet you."

Mrs. Owl replies, "We are very glad to meet you, too, my dear. I understand why you are quite concerned. I will tell you; we do keep an eye on Kitty while he visits our home. I am certain you know how much he loves to be out late at night. He fancies himself a great and brave explorer."

Sara tries very hard not to show shock at that news. The truth is, she is not aware that her son has been spending time outside late at night. She thought Kitty understood to stay inside until after sunrise.

Mrs. Owl's keen eyes see the surprise on Sara's face. She smiles and remembers her last brood of owlets. "It is hard to allow children the freedom to go their own way. We worry about the decisions they will make."

Mrs. Owl pauses and then continues her conversation. "Kitty is a remarkable youngster, Miss Sara. He cares for everything and everyone as if all is his responsibility, and his alone. He deserves protection."

Mr. Owl interrupts, "He cares for everything and everyone except those tasty mice. He can eat a half dozen. Oh, face it Mother, you have taken a real shine to the boy."

"Miss Sara, as you can tell, the wife makes me watch him like a hawk. Excuse the expression, ladies."

Sara giggles. "I do see."

Mrs. Owl asks, "So what adventure is Kitty on this week? Is it that fishing trawler and skiff that has been meeting out here the last couple of nights?"

Sara is amazed. "Why yes, it is! Kitty believes they are hiding dangerous evidence." Sara is excited the Owls know about the trawler and skiff. But then again, owls supposedly see and hear almost everything.

"Kitty is determined to solve the mystery. He found the skiff up at the Brown Estate and fears they work for Miss Brown's brother, Ronnie. He is the contractor doing the repairs on the dock and boathouse."

Mr. Owl breaks in again. "Nah, those two men with the skiff live past the Brown house, at the next house up the river. There is no pier at their house, so Miss Brown lets them keep their skiff at her pier."

Sara is so impressed. "You know so much already. Do you know what the skiff carries to the fishing trawler at night?"

Mrs. Owl answers, "No, not yet. They have only come here the last two nights. Papa, maybe you can take a trip to the other side of the river tonight and see what is going on over there."

Mr. Owl fluffs his wings and shakes. "Mother, I sure will be glad when nesting season is over. I must do everything around here."

Mrs. Owl scowls. Seeing that owls prefer to steal other nests in better condition instead of building their own, she hardly sees how Papa does everything around here.

"Everything, Papa? Are you the one that defends and reasons with the Bald Eagles or the Osprey that we are stealing their perfectly cared for nests each year?

I tell you what, Papa, I will take an evening flight over to the other side of the river to sit on a nice tree branch and observe things.

You stay here and once again explain to Osprey or the Bald Eagles that they must rebuild an older nest to use this season, one of their nests that we destroyed while raising our last owlets.

Or, Papa, you could stay here and build us a new nest all by yourself. And remember our past broods. Our nests must be strong enough to possibly raise four active owlets."

"I am going, I am going. I may be gone for a few hours, Momma. I may have to sit some time watching things." Mr. Owl chuckles and ruffles his feathers.

"Goodbye Sara. It was very nice meeting you. I am sorry about the initial fright I gave you. It is my job to protect Mother and the Point. We will help watch over Kitty; Mother says so." He laughs another hearty chuckle and turns for takeoff.

Mrs. Owl calls to Mr. Owl, "While you are over at the other side of the river, Papa, do you think you can pick up some rabbit fur from Rabbit Forest for our nest?"

Mrs. Owl explains to Sara. "Rabbit Forest is heavily wooded and just west of Hidden Cove."

Mr. Owl grumbles. "Rabbit fur, indeed. And what is wrong with the skunk fur I brought you?"

"Papa, skunk may be your favorite meat, but rabbit is my favorite fur."

As Mr. Owl leaves, he turns his head around and yells back, "And really, Mother, four owlets? What is wrong with just one or two owlets? Don't you think you work me hard enough as it is?"

Sara looks at Mr. and Mrs. Owl with sincere appreciation. "I want to thank you for helping keep an eye on my son. I know he is safe with you. I am certain he will see you soon. Apparently, it may be after I fall asleep."

Both mothers giggle in mutual understanding and with admiration. They make plans to see each other soon, and Sara heads home to sleep.

Thursday, a few hours before sunrise

Kitty's eyes open wide. It is a long time until sunrise, but he is eager to go. He nudges Momma and asks, "May I go see Mr. and Mrs. Owl? I have important questions for them."

A sleeping Momma answers, "Certainly," and quickly falls back into deep sleep.

Kitty stops in the kitchen to eat a snack and then runs all the way to the Point. Once there, he searches for Mr. and Mrs. Owl. Not finding them, he lies down and gazes towards the hidden cove. *Maybe the Owls are out hunting.*

Soon, Kitty sees Mrs. Owl soar above the Point. She sweeps down under a tree and plucks something off the ground. With her talons gripping it tightly, she flaps her almost five-foot wings twice and easily glides to the spot just in front of Kitty.

This is the closest Mrs. Owl has ever been to Kitty. Mr. Owl has yet to return from the hidden cove across the river. She needs to see why Kitty has chosen to come out here so much later tonight than usual.

"Should not you be in bed, Master Kitty? Does your mother know you are out here?" Mrs. Owl asks.

"Yes, Ma'am, she does. Wow that was some impressive flying, Mrs. Owl." Kitty looks at the mighty bird with the utmost respect. "You fly real pretty, the prettiest of all the owls I have ever seen. I have seen many owls in flight during my adventures."

Mrs. Owl's cheeks blush just a bit, and she sweetly thanks Kitty before swallowing her snack, tail, and all.

"Mrs. Owl, I was so tired from yesterday's trip to Browns Bay, I slept through most of the night. Did you see the trawler and skiff last night Mrs. Owl? Did I miss those human varmints?"

"Yes, Master Kitty, the four suspects were all here around midnight. They repeated the same events as the two nights prior. In addition, that same skiff carrying the man in the black hat returned to Browns Bay. Fortunately, my dear, this time I followed. That tall man in the black hat pays little attention to anything that goes on around him."

"That sure is true, Mrs. Owl." Kitty remembers the same man steering his skiff so close to the Old Dock but not paying any attention to Kitty being there.

"You followed the varmint in the black hat, Mrs. Owl?" Kitty is delighted, and he starts jumping and dancing around in circles. "Will you tell me what happened? Can you tell me, please?"

The magnificent looking Owl nestles into a comfortable position and tells her story. "Well, Master Kitty, as I recall, the tall man in the black hat cut the skiff's engine as he turned into Browns Bay. He quietly drifted to the pier and docked. Then he spent a good amount of time cleaning the skiff.

When finished, he put a sack on his back and slowly walked past that odd looking home on wheels where the workers stay. To my surprise, Master Kitty, that man walked straight on into the woods."

Mrs. Owl has a most different but very elegant way of speaking. Kitty listens carefully to understand her accent. He is very glad she speaks slowly.

She continues, "I certainly thought it most unusual that he decided to walk straight into the dark woods when a perfectly usable and moonlit lane was in front of him."

"Yes, that does seem very suspicious." Kitty agrees.

"Now Master Kitty, of course, I followed your varmint suspect via treetop to treetop. He paid no attention to me. He followed a narrow path until he reached a parked black truck tucked tightly in the trees."

Kitty's eyes open wide. "The black truck, Mrs. Owl, you found the black truck!"

"Yes, I did," states Mrs. Owl. "Furthermore, he drove that black truck backwards through the woods and into the neighboring yard! He parked his truck and entered the house he lives in."

"Wow," is the only word Kitty can manage. He does not want to miss one single word Mrs. Owl speaks.

Mrs. Owl appreciates Kitty's attentiveness and continues her story. "There is a trace of an old road between the neighbor to the west and Miss Brown's estate. However, the woods in that section are dense with briar patches and large brush. The man with the long, full beard rides with the tall man in the black hat. They drive the truck as far as possible into the woods. Then they walk the remaining way to the skiff at Miss Brown's dock."

Kitty interrupts. "Excuse me, Mrs. Owl. The black truck has been hiding in the woods?"

Mrs. Owl agrees, "Yes, when he takes his skiff out at night, he parks his truck in the woods. He and the man with the long, full beard walk the rest of the way to the skiff. When he returns, he is alone. A few hours later, the man with the long, full, beard, is dropped off at their house by one of the men from the trawler."

Kitty lowers his forehead and eyebrows in contemplation. "So, the human varmint in the black hat does not work for Mr. Ronnie Brown. And he lives next door to Miss Brown. I am very glad because Miss Brown and her brother, Ronnie Brown, do not act like varmints."

Mrs. Owl looks to the river and smiles. "Here comes Papa. I do hope he has my rabbit fur. He loves skunk meat and wants to bring me their furs. But rabbit is my favorite. It is the softest and best fur for our nest. Rabbits over on the other side of the river are so much larger and softer than the ones we have here."

Mr. Owl swoops over their nesting tree and drops something into the nest. Mrs. Owl shrills in delight, "Oh Papa, you remembered!"

He soars to the ground and joins Mrs. Owl and Kitty. "Like I would forget! Mother, your new furs are of the highest quality found in Rabbit Forest. And please note I said furs. I brought you two rabbit pelts."

Mr. Owl explains to Kitty, "Kitty, Rabbit Forest is beside and behind what you call hidden cove. Hidden Cove! That is as good a name as any. We will now call that cove Hidden Cove!"

Kitty is pleased. "Mr. Owl, Hidden Cove? You have been to Hidden Cove? And did you find evidence?"

Mrs. Owl announces, "I will see you two later. I have a nest to tend!"

Mr. Owl steps closer to Mrs. Owl. "Your nest needs to wait, Mother. We have a dire situation to discuss."

Kitty gasps with fear. Mrs. Owl looks up at her nest with worry. The fish are not awake yet, but a few dozen hiding and curious woodland creatures start whispering to each other. Raccoons, possum, rabbits, squirrels, and others all wait for Mr. Owl to explain what a very grave situation must be coming to Magnolia Grove.

6 ~ IMPORTANT MEETINGS

"My children! We need that river to catch and clean food. Oh my, we must have a healthy river!"

Kitty arrives home very tired from his nighttime adventure. *It is too early to wake anyone, and I do need a little nap.* He falls asleep within seconds after jumping into bed.

It is still an hour before sunrise, and Sara wakes to a staring Kitty, eager to start their day. "Good morning, Momma! I have a busy day today. Can we start extra early this morning?"

After a small yawn and a moment of stretching, she wakes enough to reply. "You will have breakfast, a bath, and lessons before you take off anywhere, young man. You know you also owe Captain a report."

Kitty gets excited. "Yes, Momma, I must tell Captain about the varmints." He thinks carefully and begins to tell Momma his story.

The kitchen is still dark when Kitty and Momma enter the kitchen. Momma notices that Kitty is not throwing food out of his bowl in all directions. "Captain will be pleased to see your eating manners have improved, Kitty."

"I am trying, Momma. But what will Grace feed the little birds if she does not have my messes to give them?"

Momma frowns and smiles at the same time. "Kitty you know perfectly well Captain and Grace have an entire winter supply of critter food. You discovered it when you dove into an open bucket and spread it all over the shed and into the yard. The critters invaded the area and ate well for a week."

Kitty remembers. "Oh yes, that was fun. I am sorry."

Captain whistles as he enters the room and pours a cup of coffee. He chuckles, "Well good morning. You two are up early. I bet Kitty has something to do with it."

Captain sits and looks at Kitty with a most curious face. "Sara, things are odd enough around here, and now Kitty is keeping his food in his bowl. Please tell me, what will the little critters eat?"

"Oh Captain, Kitty said the same thing! But do not put ideas in his head. He is trying so hard." They both cannot help but giggle.

"What a good boy, Kitty!" Captain praises.

Kitty finishes breakfast and tells Momma how he and Max followed the path to the Brown Estate. Kitty decides, for now, not to mention the angry squirrel gang. *Momma will want to meet them. I must keep her safe.*

He explained about the boathouse and campsite. "Momma, MadmanMax says the entire boathouse looks too stinking clean. He could still smell that nasty varmint smell in the boathouse that I smelled, too."

Momma frowns, "Do you have to pick up so much of the poor speaking habits and language of MadmanMax, Kitty?"

"Yes, Momma; I mean, no Momma." Kitty then explains how two of the varmints left Browns Bay in the skiff and then crossed the river towards Hidden Cove. Sara explains the details to Captain.

He laughs and shakes his head. "I knew that huge mess Hope and I found in her boathouse looked like something Kitty would leave behind."

"Captain," Sara carefully continues, "I also had a meeting with Mr. and Mrs. Owl last night. To my surprise, it turns out they are indeed friends of Kitty and protectors of Magnolia Grove."

Kitty dances in delight. "Meow, you already met Mr. & Mrs. Owl, Momma? That is why you let me go to the Point so late last night!"

Momma's eyes open very large. "I did? I let you go to the Point in the middle of the night? Oh, my. I must have been dreaming. I admit, I felt much better after visiting the Owls."

Captain laughs. "What did the Owls tell you when you visited, Sara?"

"The Owls said the tall man with the black hat and the man with the long, full beard live in the next house past Miss Brown. They keep a skiff at Miss Brown's dock."

This time Captain looks surprised. "So, two of the men Kitty saw Tuesday night must be renting the Stephens' place."

Kitty realizes Captain is taking him very seriously. Looking into Captain's eyes, Kitty clearly and quietly states, "Evidence."

Captain and Sara smile. "His vocabulary is improving, Sara." The proud Captain, in a very astonished tone, continues. "Evidence is a three-syllable word, Sara."

Sara smiles with a touch of concern. "Yes, he is learning fast, but it is a little worrisome."

Sara directs them back on target, "Kitty says Mr. and Mrs. Owl told him that Miss Brown knows the tall man with the black hat personally. She lets him dock his skiff at her pier. There is no pier where he lives next door. Neither he nor the man with the long, full beard work for Ronnie Brown."

"Well, that is a relief," Captain notes. "It looks like the Brown family is not involved."

Sara agrees. "Captain, when I left Mrs. Owl, she had sent Mr. Owl over the river to investigate Hidden Cove. Mrs. Owl was still waiting for him to return with his report."

Kitty interrupts, "Meow, Momma, please tell Captain what Mr. Owl found over on Hidden Cove."

"Tell Captain what, Kitty?" Momma asks. What do you know about Mr. Owl and Hidden Cove?"

"Oh meow, I got so excited I forgot to tell you Momma. This morning, I was on the Point when Mr. Owl returned from Hidden Cove with his report and with Mrs. Owl's rabbit furs. You see Momma, skunk is Mr. Owl's favorite meat, but rabbit is Mrs. Owl's favorite fur."

While Kitty continues eating, Momma explains to Captain what Kitty said.

"Rabbit fur. Did you say your Mrs. Owl has a favorite fur? Will someone tell me what this has to do with our varmints? In addition, where is this Hidden Cove?"

Sara explains that Kitty calls the cove on the other side of the river Hidden Cove because it is only visible from the mouth of the Mobjack Bay and Magnolia Grove. "Hidden Cove is the cove Kitty's human varmints come in and out of at night,

Captain. And Rabbit Forrest is beside and behind Hidden Cove. Mr. Owl gets Mrs. Owls favorite nesting material from Rabbit Forest."

Captain refills his coffee. "I see. OK, so what did Mr. Owl discover and share with you about Hidden Cove, Kitty?"

Momma explains, and Kitty sits up tall. He knows this is going to be one of the most important conversations of his life. He must make Captain and Momma understand. "Well," Kitty clearly states. Then he turns to Momma, "Meow, we have a dire situation to discuss."

Momma reaches out to soothe her worried and anxious son. "OK, Kitty, we are listening."

"Meow, Momma. Mr. Owl was at Hidden Cove sitting in the trees when the varmint skiff docked at its old pier. A big van pulled up close to the shore. Two men removed many crates from the van and handed them to the tall man with the black hat and the man with the long, full beard aboard the skiff. Then the van left, meow!"

Sara leans closer to Kitty, intensely listening. *Captain needs to understand, too!*

"Meow! Mr. Owl said the men in the van seemed afraid of the crates, for they wore thick and heavy looking plastic smelling clothes. They acted nervously while whispering and looking around a lot. Meow!"

Sara explains to Captain details of the events so far. He listens carefully and replies, "I understand questioning their actions and being concerned. But, Sara, I do not understand what dire situation exists."

"Kitty, please tell us, is there more information that is important to know?" Momma awaits an answer.

"Yes, Momma, there is. You had better sit down."

Momma stares at Kitty, and she sees how serious he is. "I am sitting down, Kitty, and so is Captain. Please continue."

"Last night, Mr. Owl came back from Hidden Cove with a dire concern to discuss with both of us. And Mr. Owl says it is most urgent I tell Captain.

Plants between the pier and where the van parks are vanishing at Hidden Cove. There is no grass or weeds. Many bushes and several trees are dying."

Good, they are paying close attention. This is very important. Kitty continues.

"Meow! The worst part is that many local birds and land animals must move, Momma. Birds are building their nests in new places. The resident animals do not want their children around that dangerous cove! In addition, dead fish have washed up on shore. Animals are becoming homeless, Momma!"

Sara gasps in horror. The look on her face startles Captain. "OK, Sara. I could only understand a very little of that. Tell me. What did Mr. Owl say?" He shakes off any potential insanity for him asking a cat what an owl said.

After Sara explains Mr. Owl's discovery, Captain speaks with worry in his voice. "This is indeed a dire situation, Kitty. I am very proud of you for recognizing those varmints. And that evidence you discovered is poison. It is very bad stuff, Kitty, and true evidence!"

Captain sips his coffee and thinks on the magnitude of what he has just learned. "Sara, I have been surprised by the many things you have shared with me during our friendship. Now I find our very own Great Horned Owls, the Bubo virginianus, are truly as wise as the old legends write. Are you all special, Sara, or could it be that Magnolia Grove makes animals special?"

Captain does not wait for an answer. "Kitty, first, I want you to thank Mr. and Mrs. Owl for me and for all of Magnolia Grove. However, in addition, I have a very important job for you.

You need to get word to the sea and land creatures to stay away from Hidden Cove until it is safe again. Rod and I will seek evidence that the authorities can use to catch those men."

Momma, as always, explains the missing details to Kitty. He is very relieved that Captain is going to help. "Meow, I will, Captain. Meow."

Captain picks up Kitty. "In honor of Kitty's bravery, the Point between the Marsh and East Cove will now be named Kitty Point!"

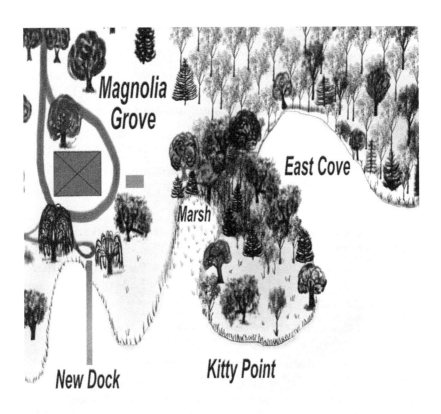

Momma explains to Kitty the good news. Kitty puffs his chest out with pride and clearly shouts, "Yay, meow. Yes! Yes! Thank you, Captain!"

Momma looks at her happy son. "Oh, go on now, and meet with Mr. and Mrs. Owl, Kitty. Try to find time to send Billy off on the school bus, too. And be careful!"

Kitty runs like the wind to Kitty Point. He shouts, "Mr. Owl and Mrs. Owl are you here? Mr. Owl and Mrs. Owl, are you up there in the trees? There is poison! Hello!"

From a distance, Kitty hears, "My goodness, Master Kitty, I am here. I am coming." Kitty spots Mrs. Owl high in her tree. She stretches, shakes out her feathers, and with ease, she gracefully soars down to the ground beside Kitty.

"Mrs. Owl, Captain sent me with important news."

Mr. and Mrs. Owl have quietly watched and listened to Captain and Kitty's mother talk many times. Unlike MadmanMax, the wise Owls understand what they say.

Wise Mrs. Owl sees the serious look on Kitty's face. With a soft voice, she asks, "Did you say the human named Captain sent you? This must be important!"

She jumps up on a log, lifts her head to the sky and yells, "Hoot, hoot!" She pecks her beak on the log, "Peck, peck, peck... Peck, peck, peck! Hoot, hoot! Papa!" she yells.

From a distance, Mr. Owl hears the urgency of Mrs. Owl's distress call.

"Hoot, hoot, hoot," yells Papa. "I am coming!" Within seconds, powerful Mr. Owl stands in front of them and defends the area. "Where is the danger, Mother?"

"The Captain of Magnolia Grove sent Master Kitty to talk to us," she explains. "It must be extremely important for him to wake us so early in the morning. And I was just falling asleep."

Mr. and Mrs. Owl both look at Kitty and then each other. It is clear Kitty is anxious to talk. He can barely sit still. Mrs. Owl softly speaks. "Go ahead, Master Kitty."

Kitty stands tall and proud. "Captain is very alarmed about the land and water at Hidden Cove. But first, he wants to thank you for sharing the danger you discovered there. He also thanks you on behalf of all the creatures here on Kitty Point and the remainder of Magnolia Grove Estate."

Despite the serious nature of Kitty's visit, Mrs. Owl manages a smile. "Kitty Point? I see. Your Captain is very gracious to send such a message Master Kitty. Thank him for us, please."

"Yes, Ma'am, I will."

"Can we worry about etiquette later, Mother?" Mr. Owl is back on subject. He turns to Kitty.

"Kitty, you said the thank you from your Captain is the first thing to tell us. What else is there, Kitty?"

"Captain says those crates the men handle are full of poison. Captain requests that we all reach the land animals, the birds, and the sea creatures to warn them to stay away from Hidden Cove and those boats until it is safe."

Kitty sees worry on Mrs. Owl's face, as does Mr. Owl.

Kitty adds hope. "Captain is working on a plan to catch those varmints and save all of you and the river. But he is going to need everyone's help!"

"Papa," Mrs. Owl sweetly interrupts, "maybe we need a Great Gathering of all the leaders. They can help spread the alarming news to all the other creatures."

Mr. Owl scratches his head as he paces in circles. He stops and agrees, "Yes, we need a Great Gathering! They can then spread the word to their friends and families!"

Kitty stands tall. "We can save everyone!"

Mr. Owl agrees. "OK, have Mr. and Mrs. Terrapin contact their network and notify all water creatures over near Rabbit Forest of the danger. Those wise turtles have been here for many years. They have the network connections to reach the sea animals quickly.

I will arrange a detail of birds to spread the news to the land creatures over near Hidden Cove. We will also notify any leaders that can make the journey that we will have a Great Gathering here one hour before sunset."

Mrs. Owl adds the final touch. "Papa, you know how frightened or territorial some will be. To ensure success, we will offer protection and safe passage to all that help."

In agitation, Mr. Owl flaps his spread-out wings and rises four feet off the ground and down again. "Mother, I will be flying to the next county for our food. But, well, yes, Mother, I guess we can do that for more cooperation."

Of the many local animals hiding among the bushes and listening, Mrs. Raccoon first chatters out in support.

"My children are to be born here come spring, and we need that river to catch our food and clean it. Oh my, we must have a healthy river! What can we do to help?"

The animals start talking amongst themselves. They agree they must help the Owls and the human Captain save the river and their homes. Of course, the offering of protection and safe passage to those that help is a welcome bonus, too.

"Mother, all the birds from the osprey to the cardinal can spread word of the danger. This is vital. At the Great Gathering, we will discuss ideas.

Find that Buck family. They will reach all the deer fast."

Mr. Owl looks very serious. "Kitty, you go through the brush and notify any small animals that may have missed the news. The raccoons, skunks, possum, rabbits, and all other land animals must know about the danger. They can help, too. Most have come to trust you."

Mr. Owl steps closer to Kitty. "Kitty, we can use MadmanMax, too. His family is huge." He lets out a chuckle.

"You know, Mother once saw Max go mad on a gigantic hawk that was about to attack his family. Locals say that hawk lost half his face and feathers that day. He has not been around here since.

In addition, Kitty, also be sure to reach that squirrel gang that tried to bully you. They can travel through their brush to inform leaders on the other side of the Field of Butterflies.

Mother told me about your bravery, Kitty. I would pity that gang if they had attacked the two of you with Mother near."

Kitty gets a look of surprise on his face. "Mrs. Owl was with us on the path? We did not see her!"

"Yes, she was there, and she told me all about it. When you were safe, she flew to the boathouse to nap and wait for you."

Mr. Owl sees that Kitty is very impressed and adds, "Mrs. Owl is the smartest owl you will ever meet, Kitty. Lucky for you, she is also the kindest.

Do not forget to tell your momma, Kitty. Miss Sara needs to be at the Great Gathering, too. She will help translate a report to the human Captain. Now go!"

"Yes, sir, I will!" Kitty runs to work the forest.

Mr. Owl affectionately looks up at Mrs. Owl in their nest. "Mother, you are correct predicting Kitty being important to us. He is getting the humans to help us save Magnolia Grove and our river."

Mrs. Owl shakes her wings and readies for flight. "I will see you this evening, Master Kitty. Goodbye for now!"

Kitty spends the next hour tirelessly running through the forest. He announces the meeting and warns of danger to every creature that can hear him. He pleads that they all do the same.

Kitty looks towards the sun. *Billy should almost be ready for school. Miss Grace depends on me to keep him safe until he gets on the bus.*

He finds Billy in his room gathering his schoolbooks. "Hi, Kitty, I am ready for school."

"Meow!"

Kitty and Billy play the entire way to Magnolia Road. They run in and out of the woods and play hide and seek. Billy throws pinecones for Kitty to learn to catch.

They are both laughing when they reach the end of the lane. They rest on the bench where Billy catches the bus.

"Everyone is talking about Annual Shoreline Cleanup Day. My teacher says everyone must keep the environment healthy.

Locals will clean the river edges and remove trash that can harm marine life and people. Captain, Rod, and I are going."

Kitty tries to understand. *I think Billy is excited about cleaning the river. Captain sure is.*

"Meow, Momma says flooding tides bring trash from everywhere. Some humans even throw trash in the river, meow! That does not seem smart. Meow!"

Kitty decides Billy is still too young to understand the dangers of Hidden Cove. He keeps the information to himself. *Billy needs protection.*

Of course, Billy would not understand anyway.

They wait for the bus. Billy pats his trumpet case with affection.

Oh yes, that thing makes a lot of noise. Despite the very unpleasant thought, Kitty can tell Billy is doing well at school. Billy gets on the bus and Kitty runs home.

Captain and Momma are working on Betty. Momma is on varmint bug duty and Captain is doing routine maintenance.

Captain looks up at Kitty and grins. "Kitty, tonight we take Betty for a night run. No varmints are leaking poison in front of our land tonight."

Momma starts explaining, but Kitty interrupts. "Momma, Captain is sure moving fast. Can we have a meeting? I have important news from Mr. and Mrs. Owl."

Momma tells Captain that the Owls sent a report. He stops.

Kitty knows his job is important. He explains about The Great Gathering and how Mr. and Mrs. Owl are offering refuge and are creating an information network. "Mrs. Owl has offered protection to all animals that help! Everyone wants to help, Captain!"

Captain closely listens as Sara interprets.

Suddenly, he sits up straight and his face smiles. "I have an idea. Maybe the birds can also follow the trawler and the van! Of course, I will never be able to tell anyone about it. Who would believe me? Sara, ask Kitty if he can get Mr. and Mrs. Owl to understand and add this to the plan."

Momma relays the message to Kitty, and he positively responds, "Meow, yes, I can. Mr. and Mrs. Owl are wise like you, Momma. They know everything."

Sara smiles at Kitty's respect for her and the Owls. "The Owls do have an extraordinary understanding of things, Captain. I am certain Kitty will have no trouble explaining things."

"That is great news, Sara."

"You return any messages the Owls might have, Kitty."

Kitty takes a deep breath. "OK Captain, meow. OK Momma, I understand. This is very important. Meow!"

Kitty starts to depart Betty. "I must go report all this to MadmanMax, meow! Oh yes, and I need to tell that mean squirrel gang we tricked, too. Mr. Owl said that leader can help."

Sara stands and demands, "Kitty, stop! Did I hear that you tricked a mean squirrel gang? Really, what is next, son?"

My big mouth did it again, and Momma sounds annoyed. Oh, no, she will want to go see them.

"It is OK, Momma," he tells her. "We made a fair deal for safe passage over their territory. Meow, I must go, Momma." Kitty tries once again to escape. This time he clears the plank and jumps onto the pier.

"Kitty," Momma sounds a little louder and a bit more irritated this time, "what fair deal could you possibly make with a mean squirrel gang?"

Feeling trapped, Kitty realizes he must tell Momma the truth. He carefully chooses his words, hoping not to upset her.

"The deal is that if those squirrels let us have safe passage between Magnolia Grove and Browns Bay, the Owls will not eat them. So, you see, it is OK now, Momma. I must go. Bye!"

Kitty giggles as he runs off the pier. He escapes before she can think of another question and stop him again.

Sara is terrified thinking about Kitty tricking a gang of squirrels. As Kitty disappears amongst the landscape and heads for the Old Dock, Sara shares her upsetting story about how MadmanMax and Kitty tricked a mean squirrel gang. Captain starts laughing. Seeing Sara's reaction, he tries to stop.

"It is not that funny, Captain." Sara frowns as her tail switches in disapproval.

7 ~ MESSAGES DELIVERED

Mrs. Owl smiles as she gently strokes Kitty's head. "You have done a remarkable job, Master Kitty. Be very proud."

—

Mr. and Mrs. Max soundly sleep on the tree limb that serves as their front porch. Their bushy tails limply hang off the limb. Kitty knows he is going to upset Max's wife, but he tries anyway not to scare her.

"Max!" he whispers. "Max!"

Kitty sighs. *Mm. They sure are sound sleepers.* "Oh, Max!!"

Mrs. Max opens one eye. Kitty freezes in place, hoping she stays calm, but she jumps high in the air and screams anyway. As she runs towards their tree den door, she yells, "Oh my! Max, that awful cat has no business here!" Within another second, she is deep inside their tree cavity.

By this time, Max is also very awake. "I see, or rather I hear, you met the Mrs. Tell me, Kid, how did it go for you?"

"Not too good, Max. Your wife certainly does not like me. She has never even met me. But, Max, she must listen to the Owl's message."

Max leaps to the ground. "The Owls sent a message, you say? Spill it, Kid."

Kitty explains the horror of the dying vegetation discovered at Hidden Cove. He tells of the important meeting tonight at Kitty Point with all the leaders. "The Owls want you at tonight's meeting, Max."

Max stands tall with a puffed-out chest, "Well, of course, Mr. and Mrs. Owl need me there."

"We have to help Captain save the Severn River!" Then Kitty tells Max of Captain's plan to have the animals help.

Max's eyes widen. "That will startle them human varmints."

"All the leaders will meet one hour before sunset on Kitty Point. We must let the squirrel gang know. And you can spread word throughout your woods, Max."

Max starts scampering about. "We cannot have that stinking poison here. It will kill everything. Let's go!" They both run along the path to the squirrel gang's territory.

Max stops and sniffs the air. "That stinking gang is close."

Kitty yells. "Come out. We are all in great danger." There is no response. He yells again. "Mr. and Mrs. Owl sent me to talk to you."

"What do you want, Cat, Squirrel? We already have a deal. You cannot break it."

"We are here to help you." Kitty slowly explains why they need to take precaution around the river until all is safe.

The leader steps out of the woods. "Why are you helping us stay safe? Why are you giving us protection from those two owls you call Mr. and Mrs. Great Horned Owl? Huh, Cat?"

"Well," Kitty quickly thinks. "You helped us by offering my friend and me passage through your territory."

The leader scratches. "Well, I guess we did help you, didn't we?"

"Anyway, this is the right thing to do. Everyone needs some protection sometimes, even you. Come to the meeting."

Kitty thinks a bit more. "Uh," *This is just a little stretch on the truth.* "Mr. Owl says you will be protected with other top leaders."

"So that Mr. Owl called me a top leader, eh? Well, I am glad he notices." The leader rises and spreads out his chest.

"He is full of himself, that joker," Max whispers.

The leader scratches again. "A cat and a squirrel, What a strange pair. Well, OK, it's a deal. We will spread the word and then see you at the meeting." The squirrels gather for discussion before scattering into the woods.

Max shakes his head. "Can we trust them stinking squirrels?"

"Probably not, Max," Kitty says. "But I believe they are so afraid of the Owls; they will do anything in hope of having Mr. and Mrs. Owl's protection."

They arrive at Max's treehouse and agree to meet later at Magnolia Cottage well before the sun hits the top of the trees. From there, Max, Kitty, and Sara will go to the Great Gathering together.

As they part company, Max has his mind on how to share all this information with his nervous wife.

When Max enters their home, Mrs. Max is already packing the family nuts. "We will go stay with my parents until we build a new home on the inland side of the estate."

"You know, Wife, we have discussed this. We very well may catch those stinking varmints before we have to move."

Mrs. Max ignores him and continues to pack.

Max shakes his head. "I do not know what good a new home will do for us if everything around us is dead. Besides, you know perfectly well, I must live near the water.

Now, I must go warn our family and friends. Then I go meet the Kid and the Owls for the big meeting. Stay calm, Wife!"

Mrs. MadmanMax scowls. "I will pack anyway. We must be prepared!"

As Max scampers down his treehouse, he hears his wife yelling, "Max, that cat is nothing but trouble!"

Kitty briskly walks towards the Point Captain named Kitty Point. He thinks over his responsibilities *I am not too young anymore!*

Kitty has notified many animals to be cautious of the varmints and poison. He has informed leaders to attend the Great Gathering tonight. Many animals in turn will now spend the rest of the day spreading the news. *Everyone must be safe.*

Kitty feels an odd feeling in his throat, almost a swelling. He walks with a tall posture and feels a deep sense of purpose.

Yes, I am all grown. A baby cannot do the important things I am doing. I am going to help save Hidden Cove, the Severn River, and Mobjack Bay. I must!

Kitty clears the path and reaches Kitty Point to find Mr. and Mrs. Owl asleep near their nest. Kitty does not want to wake them, for it will be the second time Kitty wakes them today. However, this message is crucial, and Captain needs help.

"Kitty," a grumpy Mr. Owl bellows, "do you have to make so much noise? Why are you here?"

"I am sorry Mr. Owl, but I have an important message from Captain. Maybe you better wake Mrs. Owl."

Mrs. Owl unruffled her feathers and stretched out her massive wings. "Well, Papa, Master Kitty may have been loud, but your voice alone is the one that woke me!"

Mrs. Owl looks Kitty over carefully. "Master Kitty, I do hope you are getting enough rest. Now tell us, what news do you have?"

Kitty stands tall. He knows how important this message is, for Captain is depending on him.

Kitty calls out, "Captain needs your help, please."

The mighty couple swoops towards the ground. Flapping their giant wings just twice, together they gracefully land, standing magnificently in front of Kitty.

"Wow." Kitty admiringly states.

Mr. Owl, now more awake, is also more agreeable. "Kitty, is there more to tell?"

"Yes!" Kitty replies. "Captain wants to ask if you and the others can follow the van and that trawler tonight. Captain needs to know where they go. They must not escape!"

Kitty further explains that Rod is going to drive his truck over to Hidden Cove where the van meets the skiff and investigate for evidence. Rod may also be able to follow the van.

Mr. Owl thoughtfully replies. "Your Rod may need more than just himself to keep an eye on that trawler and van. I better send a detail of birds over to keep an eye on him."

Mrs. Owl agrees. "Yes, Papa, he is young and can easily get into trouble. He just started attending a famous school, you know."

Kitty jumps up and down in glee. "Yes!" Kitty squeals.

The wise Mrs. Owl leans forward and looks down into Mr. Owl's eyes. The Great Horned Owls have large and mighty males, but the female owls are even larger and mightier.

"OK Mother, OK, I hear you. At the gathering, we will make plans to keep an eye on that trawler and van from the air. We may be able to help if we follow those human varmints, to quote Kitty." Mr. Owl chuckles.

Mr. Owl suddenly remembers who Rod is. "Oh, no, Mother. Is Rod that young man with the annoying dog? That dog chases everything that moves, including leaves."

"Oh yes," Kitty says. "That is Bear. He is really annoying."

Mr. Owl shakes his head in disapproval. "Mother, that dog even chases his own tail. I do not want him around tonight."

"Papa now is not the time to worry about a harmless dog."

"Well, Mother, that dog starts running and forgets to stop. He is noisy, too." Mr. Owl complains.

Kitty looks up at the Owls with the utmost adoration and respect. He then steps up and assures Mr. Owl.

"Bear will be left at home this evening, Mr. Owl. Rod must be very careful. We must all be very careful. Those varmints are very dangerous."

Mr. Owl shakes his feathers and swells almost twice his size. "I can be very dangerous, too, Kitty. Sometimes, I take them out in two seconds. Other times, I take them out by simply staring. It is very easy."

"Papa, watch the bragging about your fighting skills and talents."

Mr. Owl grunts. "Mother, we have a very busy evening ahead of us. With all those different animals together, we cannot be certain all will go as planned. We must be rested with clear minds."

Mrs. Owl smiles as she gently strokes Kitty's head. "You have done a remarkable job, Master Kitty. Be very proud. Now you must go home and report to Captain. Get plenty of rest today for tonight's Great Gathering. You will need it!"

It is late morning, and the sun glistens through the trees. It seems to amplify the birds' chatter. *The birds are busy telling everyone about Hidden Cove, making sure all know of the threat of the dangerous poison.*

Kitty heads home to Magnolia Grove feeling better, knowing everyone is helping. He has done his very best.

Entering the house, his stomach growls for food. After eating, he realizes the house is empty. *Where is Captain and Momma? I will check next door. Captain needs a report!*

Kitty squeals when he sees Rod's truck in Grace's driveway. *What is Rod doing home early on a Thursday?*

Bear plays outside in front of the house. He laughs at seeing Kitty. *Bear is always happy, but he rarely pays attention to much of anything.*

"Meow, we have big problems in the river, Bear. There is a big meeting tonight."

Bear stops and stares at Kitty. "On such short notice? Is this after dinner? Can we have dinner first?"

"No, meow," Kitty snaps, "the meeting is before dinner and never mind. Meow, you must stay home with Billy. You cannot chase any animals anyway."

"Then why go?" Bear asks without further interest.

"Bear, this is serious. We have human varmints on the river! We all need a healthy river. Don't you want Rod to be safe?"

Bear replies by chasing his own shadow and then running after a leaf. He completely forgets about Kitty.

Kitty jerks his tail back and forth in agitation. "That dog!"

Inside Grace's kitchen, Kitty finds Momma, Captain, and Rod sitting at the table. He runs to Rod and jumps on his lap.

"Rod!" Kitty clearly squeals in delight. He knows Rod will help save the animals and the river.

Momma and Captain look at each other with shocked faces. Both feel relief that Rod does not seem to notice Kitty clearly speaking his name.

Rod pets Kitty and gently speaks. "Well, there you are. Are you going to help us catch the bad people, Kitty?"

Surprised Captain accidentally speaks aloud to Sara. "I called Rod early this morning. We need him home to help us track down those criminals. We need all the help we can get."

Rod looks suspiciously at Captain. "Captain, are you talking to Sara, to Kitty, or to a ghost?"

"No, he is talking to me." Grace laughs as she refills her coffee cup. She comes from behind Rod and joins the group at the table. "It sounds like we have a plan."

Sara and Captain look at each other strangely. Captain is grateful that Grace jumped in to save the situation, no matter how mistaken all this must seem.

"Meow, we have a plan, Momma? Meow!" Kitty gets excited. He is trying hard to keep up with their conversations.

They talk so fast! I am just learning English!

Grace smiles and recaps. "Rod will drive to Hidden Cove and wait for the van to deliver the poison-filled crates to the skiff. Earlier today, he found a safe spot to hide his truck and hopefully take some photos of the van, the license plate, and the men. He may even get a chance to follow the van.

Kitty can go with you."

That is a good idea. Rod needs protection.

Captain laughs. "Rod, you have been wanting to use my new night vision binoculars and camera since I purchased them. Get us some good night photos. And Rod, you remember to be careful. Take no chances."

"I will, Captain!" Rod smiles and heads for Captain's new camera and binoculars.

Kitty starts to speak, but Grace swiftly offers a discreet pet on his nose.

Grace continues. "Meanwhile, the weather is perfect to take Betty out for a run. Captain will anchor her down in the East Cove at Kitty Point and spy on the trespassing varmints."

Captain interjects, "Yes, or we may have need to follow the trawler. If we do, with good weather, enough distance, and Betty's lights off, we might be able to follow that boat unnoticed. We will see."

Chuckling, Captain continues. "We may be out all night, Grace. How about making us some sandwiches and snacks?"

Captain grabs some clean rags from the dryer and announces, "I am going to meet Ronnie Brown at the Boat Barn and then head over to check Betty. See you later!"

Kitty stays behind with Grace in the kitchen. She looks at Kitty and places her hands on her hips. "So, young man, you can say Rod's name, too. Your vocabulary is growing."

Kitty jumps onto a chair, looks up to Miss Grace with tenderness, and gives her a very big smile. "Rod!" He squeals. "Rod!"

"I know you are happy to see Rod, but you must be careful." Grace tries to make Kitty understand. She pets her good friend and speaks softly. "Please do not let people know your secret, Kitty. It may not be safe. We will tell the others as soon as I find the right time. Sam will think I am crazy."

"Yes." Kitty says quietly and thinks about what Miss Grace just said. *Just Momma and Captain know. Oh yeah, and Max. And Mr. and Mrs. Owl. And… Oh my, I had better tell Miss Grace. I will tell her as soon as I find the right time.*

"Good." Grace praises Kitty. "Now, try to remember."

Kitty falls into a deep sleep while Grace makes chicken sandwiches and cheese dip. She adds her special salad recipe of tomato, cucumber, onion, and feta cheese. She packs plenty of grapes and cookies for dessert. Then, Grace adds a bag with kitty food and a variety of kitty snacks.

Grace talks to herself. "That should keep the four of them fed tonight. In the morning, they can all come home for breakfast."

Shortly, Sara returns to look for Kitty. She finds him asleep on a large pillow in the corner of Grace's kitchen. She decides to join him.

Kitty stirs and opens his eyes. "Tell Captain the Owls understand what to do, Momma."

"I will. You have done well, Son."

They both fall asleep. A long rest is just what they both need before the important Great Gathering.

While Kitty and Sara sleep

Ronnie Brown arrives at the Boat Barn. Captain greets him.

"Good afternoon, Captain. I have an estimate for your new roof. I assume you will want to buy materials yourself."

Captain looks over the estimate. "Why, this is great, Ronnie. You are well within my budget. Start the work whenever you are ready. The building supply store has my shingle choice. You can tell them what and how much to order and deliver at any time."

"I will stop by there today, Captain."

Once in the truck, Ronnie reaches for his phone and grins. "Hello, Mr. Green! I have good news. We have the repair job at Magnolia Grove. It is going to buy us the additional time we may need to get our other mission done. How do you like that for luck?"

Ronnie listens. "You mean, the neighbor with the boat barn, Captain Sam? Why no, he has not asked me any questions. He just talks about his new roof estimate. With luck, you will be able to clean up this mess soon. I will call you later."

Momentarily, Captain answers his ringing phone. "Hello… Yes, Mark. Thanks for calling me back. What did you find out?"

Captain is relieved. "I see. I am very glad to hear you agree we have criminal activity!" He then listens carefully.

"OK, Mark, but, well, there seems to be a lot of threatening activity developing here."

Captain sighs. "I understand what you mean, but things are serious here. I guess there is little we can do until you and the authorities arrive tomorrow. We will talk later."

Captain hangs up and thinks over the situation.

Captain finds Rod to discuss his conversation with Mark. "Rod, something tells me that we do not have the time to wait until the authorities arrive tomorrow. Tomorrow may be too late."

"So, we continue as planned, Captain?"

"Yes, we do, Rod."

"Good evening, gentlemen," Mrs. Owl politely nods to the
bucks. "Thank you for coming."

MadmanMax sits in a tree and watches through Grace's kitchen window. Kitty and his mother enter the kitchen, eat, and finally come outside. All together, they will go to Kitty Point and the Great Gathering.

"You two are going to make us late." The agitated squirrel complains as he jumps to the ground. "Mrs. Owl needs us to keep things calm until Mr. Owl returns. With all those stinking tempers together, it won't be long before one of them busts a jaw, loses an eye, or gets a limb chewed off. That is if most of them are on good behavior."

Kitty's mother does not look amused. She whispers, "Really, Kitty, does Mr. MadmanMax have to be so crude?"

Kitty thinks a few seconds. "But Momma isn't he correct? That is a lot of animals together at one time."

Sara sees how much Kitty admires his friend. She clears her throat and for her son's benefit, she directs her conversation to the squirrel. "Well, uh, that is excellent thinking, Mr. MadmanMax. We better hurry, so we can do just as you say."

Max looks Sara over very closely and looks at Kitty. "Ah, I guess we have a little time. Let's all remember we are a team, and we can do this! We will follow you, Miss, Ms., uh, Mrs. – just what do I call you?" MadmanMax realizes he does not know her name. She knows his.

Sara sounds polite and smiles as she lowers her head to a nod. "My name is Sara. It is nice to finally meet you properly." She begins to think that this squirrel may indeed be a good friend for Kitty. He seems smart, too.

MadmanMax reacts to her formal introduction poorly. "In this serious and dangerous situation, I see no reason to think about proper anything." He stops suddenly as Kitty's eyebrows lower to a frown. Sara's mouth drops open and her eyes widen.

The squirrel thinks fast. "Oh, I'm a bit jittery. That was too stinking much. This meeting is big. Anything could happen."

MadmanMax clears his throat and tries his best to make things better for Kitty. "Well, uh, thank you, Miss Sara. It is very nice to meet you, uh, properly, too." He looks uncomfortable.

"Kitty and friends call me Max. You can call me Max, too, uh, please." Max relaxes as he feels that surely the worst of this properness thing is behind him.

Sara appreciates Max's valiant effort and nods with a gracious and understanding smile. "Why thank you, Max. I will."

As they walk on towards Kitty Point, Kitty leans over to Momma and whispers, "See Momma, Max is a good squirrel. He has just never been to school or had lessons."

"OK," Max jumps in front. "From here on, watch every step, but be calm. Mrs. Owl wants everyone to feel welcome. After all, we do need cooperation from all."

As they continue to follow the wooded path to Kitty Point, Max mutters, "That Owl dame better know what she is doing."

Kitty defends Mrs. Owl. "Mr. Owl says she is the smartest owl we will ever know!"

"I hope you are right, Kid."

The path soon opens to Kitty Point. Trees spatter the clearing, and Kitty notices more birds in the trees than normal.

Mrs. Owl is already on watch, perched on her favorite tree limb. She watches the oddly matched trio approach her and is pleased to see them arrive early for the Great Gathering.

She waits for Papa's return from Rabbit Forrest and Hidden Cove. He went over the river to create a network of leaders to share information. Many of them will join the Great Gathering tonight. They all must work together to save their homes.

Tonight, Mr. and Mrs. Owl want everyone to understand that moving to a new location is only a temporary fix. No place will be safe if these criminals continue poisoning the nearby land and waters.

Another major issue of the meeting is explaining that the humans at Magnolia Grove are helping them. The animals also must do their part and help, so that they all may one day return to Hidden Cove.

Kitty, Max, and Sara stand guard. They make a triangle around Mrs. Owl's tree. She addresses them. "Papa will return soon. I will most certainly be glad, for the leaders and others will begin to gather."

Max circles the group and reminds them to be attentive. "Look alive everybody and keep your eyes open."

Mrs. Owl turns her head towards the woods. Four of the Big Buck family clear the trees and enter the clearing on the Point. Kitty can feel the ground shake each time their hoofs step to the ground. As the large male deer slowly march towards Mrs. Owl, they turn their heads and enormous antlers from side to side, nodding in peace to those they pass.

Kitty gasps at their size. They are much larger than the coyote he once fought to save Miss Grace. *I thought that coyote was huge but look at them!*

Mrs. Owl greets the Bucks. "If you would be so kind as to take your positions, we will start soon. Our lives depend on all of us tonight."

"On point!" One of the Bucks bellows orders to the other three. They separate to the corners of the gathering area, to help ensure every creature stays on their very best behavior.

Sara leans over to her son. "The deer have always been good to us. That is the eldest Buck. The other three are a son and two grandsons."

As the eldest buck passes, he looks over and notices Max. "Well, hello, Max. It is good to see you here. How is the Mrs. doing? Am I still her least favorite neighbor?"

"Yeah, she still has her hair frizzed over waking up with you digging up her hidden pecan and hickory nuts."

"Gee, Max, I did not know those nuts belonged to anybody." The big powerful buck bows his head.

Max laughs. "Ah, she forgets half of the places she buries her nuts anyway."

"Maybe she will forget about me taking them, too."

Max thinks. "Well, maybe, but I doubt it."

Kitty laughs. "Max, I thought your wife only dislikes me!"

"Nah, Kid, you are not that different. She dislikes almost everybody outside of the family and close friends."

The ground trembles as Mr. Buck passes and goes to the area he is to protect, the area closest to Mrs. Owl.

Kitty is amazed. "Meow, Momma, I have never met the Bucks before. However, one of the mother deer let me play with her babies. Their little babies are not so little either, Momma."

"Baby deer are called fawns, and Mother deer are doe."

Mr. and Mrs. Raccoon are the first smaller animals to come to the woods' edge. Mr. Raccoon yells behind him into the woods, "Come on out for the meeting. Everything is fine."

Animals peek out from behind trunks of trees and from under bushes. One of the skunk family, protected by the cover of a thick bush, speaks out. "That is easy for you to say, Raccoon. You are not the Owl's favorite meat!"

The Rabbits speak from behind the skunks. "How would you like to be the Owl's favorite fur for lining an owlet nest?"

"Momma, they sure are correct! I told you so!"

Next, the possum slowly emerges to the woods' edge. Mrs. Possum sounds cranky. "You have us up early tonight, for we normally sleep until after dark. Could this meeting be a trick?" She hisses and looks around at her many enemies.

"Nah," Mr. Fox steps forward. "There are too many animals here for this to be a trick. This is just as Mr. and Mrs. Owl said, the calling of a Great Gathering. We all know what this means. The rule for today is to meet in peace."

Mr. Fox then shows his teeth. He growls. "But tomorrow is a different day, possum."

His group of foxes, a skulk, gather in the back of the meeting area, the furthest distance from the group as possible.

Momma whispers to Kitty. "The fox generally keeps their distance. They do not seem to like crowds of any kind."

"Well look there, The Squirrel Gang is here for the meeting!" Max laughs.

The squirrels leap across the clearing and join the other small animals at the edge of the woods. As they pass, their leader exchanges positive nods with Max. "Hello Squirrel… Cat… The Squirrel Gang, eh? I think I like the sound of that."

Kitty looks up at the many birds in the trees. Gathering throughout the branches are wren, finch, chickadee, titmouse, nuthatch, sparrow, and many more.

"Momma, there are many little birds here, just like in Captain's books. I sit on Captain's desk and look at books with him, Momma. He has many bird books. It is fun.

I like little birds, Momma." Kitty's eyes marvel at the variety of birds. He sees cardinals, mockingbirds, dove, and blue jays. There are bluebirds, robins, blackbirds, and many others gathering in the trees.

Kitty notices several new owls he has never seen before. He looks at Mrs. Owl and then at the new owls. *They sure look like Mrs. Owl.*

Mrs. Owl notices Kitty staring at the younger owls and then to her. "Master Kitty, those are some of our previous born. They come to help their mother."

"They are the most handsome owlets I have ever seen, Mrs. Owl, and they look just like you."

Kitty gently rubs his mother's side. "I am helping my mother, too."

"Indeed, you are Master Kitty," Mrs. Owl says tenderly.

Suddenly, Mrs. Owl's forehead drops low. Her head turns completely backwards. She is the first to hear the unmistakable whistling shrills of the Osprey. In nature, Great Horned Owls may be their greatest enemy.

Four fearless members of the Osprey family land on the upper branches of a pine. Even though they are enemies, Mr. and Mrs. Owl had asked them to the Great Gathering. They come to help save the waters where they fish, the very waters they rely on for their livelihood.

Kitty whispers. "Momma, the Osprey just eat fish. They sure know how to catch fish a lot better than Rod and Captain." Kitty and Momma giggle thinking about Rod and Captain fishing sometimes for hours, catching few or no fish.

"And Kitty, Captain says the osprey are very good parents, too. They always take care of an orphan or a hungry fledgling."

Suddenly, all the birds fly out of the tree closest to Mrs. Owl. They scatter but swiftly circle around and settle in another neighboring tree. Almost simultaneously, four huge Bald Eagles gracefully soar in and land in the vacant and now available tree.

Kitty cannot help but admire the eagles' majestic beauty. Although they are fearful and mighty birds of prey, humans seem to like eagles very much.

Captain has stone eagles on both lane entrances to Magnolia Grove. He also has eagle pictures on his t-shirts, on the wall in his office, and in his stateroom on Betty. He also has lots of them on the paper in his wallet. Why, Captain has eagles everywhere!

Mallard Ducks and Canadian Geese land on the East Cove. Behind them, swans, known as Mute Swans, swim into view. They also live on the local shallow waters all year round.

"Momma, those huge mute swans hear really good. When they feed in the East Cove, they can even hear me walking on the point! And you should see how much they can eat. I saw them fishing last week. They caught fish after fish, and they ate for an hour!"

On the other side of the Point, at the shallow edge of the marsh, Mr. and Mrs. Terrapin poke out their heads. They have sent word to all resident fish, the blue crabs, and the dolphins.

Kitty runs down to the marshes edge and greets the turtles. "Hello Mr. and Mrs. Terrapin. You two have brought many to the meeting! Look at all those heads peeking out of the water!"

"Hello, Kitty." Mrs. Terrapin crawls out of the water. Her slow husband, Mr. Terrapin, follows. "We have informed all the water creatures we know.

After all," Mrs. Terrapin firmly states, "those that live in the water are at the greatest risk."

Several magnificent Blue Heron land. They are leery to be around so many enemies gathered near the marsh where they hunt. They see the crow, the bald eagles, foxes, hawks, and raccoons. All try to invade their nests and eat their precious eggs.

Gracefully, several White Egrets glide onto the Point. They join the Great Blue Herons.

Kitty often sees the Great Blue Herons and the White Egrets together and being friendly to each other. At night, egrets will roost with the heron, sleeping near each other, so they can warn each other of pending enemies and danger.

A great number of animals now fill the edges of the water, line the forest, and fill the trees. They are chattering about the looming danger facing their families and homes.

They wait for Mr. Owl to return from across the Severn River. He went to invite other leaders to tonight's Great Gathering.

They all cannot help but be a bit suspicious. All want to hear about the risky plan to join the humans and catch the varmints. All want to help, but wonder, is trusting humans wise?

"Hoot, hoot! Here comes Papa!" Mrs. Owl proclaims loudly. She starts dancing and hooting for her mate. She then catches herself a little embarrassed at not appearing dignified. "Mmm, excuse me," she whispers.

All chattering stops. Absolute quiet sets in as the mighty Mr. Owl approaches Kitty Point. He circles above the animals gathered and weaves through the trees filled with birds.

From the air, he reviews the impressive collection of animals both big and small from the land, the air, and the sea. Mrs. Owl and friends have done well notifying all the animals of the important Great Gathering.

Mr. Owl flaps his wings a few times and comes to what looks like a midair stop above Mrs. Owl's tree. With one more flap, he slowly floats down to her side.

"Hello, Mother. You have done well, as always." He looks upon his wife with respect deserving of a queen.

"Oh, Papa, I have been so worried about you." She returns his gazes of affection and respect. "If I ever lost you, I would wander this land alone for the rest of my life."

Mr. Owl puts out a wholesome laugh. "Do not worry, Mother, you can pick any direction you wish to start wandering. We have many children; you would not have to wander far to end your loneliness."

"Papa, really, do not make such jokes!"

Suddenly, one of the younger foxes completely forgets about the peace treaty. Tempting smells make him so hungry for a snack. To everyone's shock, he starts chasing one of the young Cottontail rabbits.

The animals gasp in horror. They know the rules of a Great Gathering. There is zero tolerance of any violent instincts.

Mrs. Cottontail screams for her children to scatter for safety. "I should have never allowed my family to stay for this meeting!" The brave mother rabbit hops towards the dangerous fox. She knows she must attract his attention to save her children. Luckily, her plan works, and the fox turns to follow her.

The fox quickly closes in on Mrs. Cottontail's heels. She realizes that most certainly, she will never see her children again. Not thinking of herself, and only worrying for their safety, she hops with all her might. She plans to lead the fox as far away from her family as possible. Her children deserve the freedom that comes with her protection.

Just before the mother rabbit reaches the brush and woods for safety, the fox catches up to her. He pounces forward with definite plans for a meal.

The silly fox pays no attention to the looming shadow overhead. Suddenly, a fierce bald eagle dives to the ground and forces itself between the fox and Mrs. Cottontail. With an angry voice, Mr. Bald Eagle peers down at him. "Great Gatherings are peace meetings, fox. Nobody breaks the rules. Nobody."

The desperate fox spins around to find another route of escape. Unfortunately, two massive hoofs pound the earth, once again blocking any safe getaway.

One of the grandson Bucks has also come to the rescue. He slowly speaks, "Let me help you, fox." He bends over and scoops up the fox with his massive antlers. He easily tosses the fox about fifteen feet. "You are out of here!" The fox rolls over and over, finally tumbling to a stop.

In fear of his own life, and with a new limp, the fox gets up and runs. He disappears into the woods. The remaining foxes look a little embarrassed and whisper amongst themselves. They are quiet throughout the rest of the meeting.

Mrs. Owl nods thanks to the buck and eagle as they return to their positions. She turns to her husband. "Papa, that fox broke our agreement. He needs to learn respect."

Kitty thinks. "Was that a varmint fox, Momma?"

"Well, yes, he was today. But remember he is young. Maybe this incident will teach him that self-discipline is important. Rules are important, Kitty."

Standing at the back of the group, two of the younger members of the Buck family rear up high onto their hind legs. When their hoofs pound down to the ground, the noise reminds all that a Great Gathering of the animals demands total respect.

Mr. Owl looks at Kitty and winks. He then turns to address the crowd. "Thank you all for coming. This is a very ominous time, and I will get straight to the important matter at hand. Animals have been reporting serious problems here off our Kitty Point and over at Hidden Cove.

I have flown over to Hidden Cove and confirmed the dire issue. There are men that drive their van to Hidden Cove at night. The men transfer crates from the van to a skiff at the dock. The bad part is that sometimes, poison leaks from some of the crates. Around the dock, dead fish are washing ashore. It looks like a ghost town over at Hidden Cove!

Mrs. Terrapin, how is evacuation going for the sea creatures?"

Mrs. Terrapin stretches her neck tall and speaks. "All creatures living in Hidden Cove have been notified to stay away until all is safe. Many of them have come here to Kitty Point to take refuge."

The river bubbles as the many sea creatures talk amongst themselves. They agree that the situation is most serious.

Mr. Owl continues. "I know many of you have seen that trawler off our land at night. After the skiff transports the crates to the trawler, the trawler goes to an unknown place out to sea. One of our jobs is to find that unknown place."

"Well at least they are taking the poison somewhere else! We do not want it here." Mr. Possum shouts.

"Mr. Opossum," Mrs. Owl feels slightly agitated at his lack of empathy and selfish response, "if they dump that poison anywhere into the waters, tide and weather can bring it right back into our river and kill us even if spilled elsewhere! We must join the good humans to stop the bad ones!!"

Mr. Owl beams with pride. He trusts his mate always knows what to say and what to do. He has no wonder why their many owlets are so intelligent and strong. Mr. Owl's attention goes back to addressing the crowd.

"Yes, we must stop the bad humans. They have already seriously harmed Hidden Cove. We do not yet know if there is any more damage elsewhere. Why, there may be damage out in our Mobjack Bay, and I fear, elsewhere."

Mr. Owl chooses his words carefully. He does not want to give away Kitty's secret. "As many of you know, I have informed the animals and humans at Magnolia Grove of our serious situation. After all, the danger is of equal concern to them, too. And we need their help."

The most loud and obvious of the Osprey family squawks and laughs aloud so all can hear. "And how do you know that, Owl? You cannot talk to humans."

"Oh no, and how will Mr. Owl explain that?" Kitty whispers to Max and his mother.

Mr. Owl carefully replies, "Osprey, I sent a message to the humans." Mr. Owl did not want to betray Kitty's secret. "They want to catch the bad humans and save the water, too. They need clean water as much as we do."

Making certain all hear him, Osprey squawks louder. "You sent a message to the humans? How? You are making all of this up. This is a trick, and you are a liar."

Mrs. Owl's dignified and graceful manner vanishes when she hears her noble husband insulted. She quickly flies over to Osprey's tree and lands face to face with the rude bird. Quickly coming to her assistance, her many owlets join her.

The Great Horned Owl knows her power, and she confronts Osprey. "My dear, first, this is a Great Gathering. Second, no one insults my husband.

Like the little fox, how would you like to go on the unprotected list? My owlets can banish you from the Point if you like." She flaps her wings as a warning.

The Osprey refuses to back down and, rather boldly, decides to further confront Mrs. Owl. "You know perfectly well it is impossible for humans and animals to understand each other. Therefore, this is a trick, and we would be fools to follow you!"

Mrs. Owl's body begins to swell almost twice her size.

Kitty has never seen Mrs. Owl lose her temper. It is clear she is preparing to attack her enemy. A war is about to begin.

"Max, Momma! Mrs. Owl is so mad she has forgotten the rules!"

Kitty runs with all his might. Climbing the tree in a few seconds, Kitty soon stands between Mr. Osprey and Mrs. Owl!

"Mr. Osprey, Sir, if you please. You are one of the mightiest leaders here at the Great Gathering, so I think you should know the whole truth. You need to know, Sir, so you can best help."

Four other ospreys immediately fly to their leader's side. The leading osprey twists his neck from side to side and confidently speaks. "What do I need to know from you, strange cat?"

"Do you agree he needs to know, Mrs. Owl?" Kitty asks.

"Well, that is up to you, Master Kitty. However, Osprey and Papa have never gotten along. He has no respect, and he will never listen. Therefore, I say banish him. Hoot, hoot, hoot!"

In response, six of Mrs. Owl's children swoop even closer to their mother. From the neighboring tree, Mr. Owl leans forward and readies for a glide-in attack. The Owl family is ready for battle.

In a whisper, Kitty implores, "Please, Mrs. Owl, give me just a minute."

Kitty shows no fear and steps closer to the mighty and upset osprey. He speaks in a very low but clear voice. He does not want the other animals to hear.

"Mr. Osprey, if you please. I am the one that delivers the messages to Captain. I can talk to humans. However, I only talk to the ones that live here on Magnolia Grove.

Sir, it is too dangerous to let other humans know. Momma says because I am so very rare and special, varmints might want to steal me!"

Kitty hangs his head a little. "All the humans at Magnolia Grove do not even know I can talk to the others. I guess I need to tell them. Do you think I should tell them, Mr. Osprey? It is not nice to keep secrets."

Mr. Osprey, maybe not so cold hearted, notices this cat is very young. He also sees Mrs. Owl's protective stance. He realizes that the Owl and the cat are too odd a pair for this to be any kind of trick. Truth becomes obvious.

"I see." Mr. Osprey whispers low and thinks. He then pats Kitty on the back. "Now you return to your friends standing next to Mrs. Owl's tree. The meeting must continue if we are to ever save the river."

Kitty looks up at the magnificent bird. "Are you and I now friends, too, Mr. Osprey?"

Realizing how brave this little cat is and how special his gift is, Mr. Osprey answers. "Why yes, I guess we are."

"This is good Mr. Osprey. My name is Kitty. I like friends. Please let me know if there is ever any help you need."

Mr. Osprey, taken aback by Kitty's politeness and generous offer, stutters for words. "Why, uh, thank you, I will. You too, you know. And I, uh, well, Kitty, I think you better be honest with your family."

"OK, Mr. Osprey, I will. It will not be easy."

Mrs. Owl smiles just a bit to see Kitty win over cranky, and ever aggravating, Mr. Osprey. She giggles and flies back to her tree. The other Owl family members disperse.

Kitty runs after Mrs. Owl, too, but not until he politely says, "Thank you for your help, friendship, and offer, Mr. Osprey!"

As Kitty reaches the Owl's tree, Mr. Owl winks down and laughs. "Good job, Kitty. Good job."

Mr. Owl continues talking to the crowd. "Listen everyone, the human Captain needs our help gathering evidence for their authorities. He is trying to find out where the poison comes from and where it goes. He has asked us to follow the bad humans in their van over at Hidden Cove. He also needs us to follow the big boat trawler after the skiff unloads the crates tonight."

The buzz of the creatures' voices, active with discussions and questions, follow. The plan comes together.

Mr. Owl brings the meeting to a close. "To all of you going with me, stay behind, please. Everyone else go spread the word and remember to be careful!"

Mrs. Owl adds the final statement. "To all of you, we say, whether you are here to help save the river we love, or are here for shelter, welcome! You are safe and have our protection."

The animals disperse with good news. They go home to share hope with their families. There is a plan to save their homes and the river they depend on for life.

Mr. Osprey and other birds stay behind to further develop a plan to help. They decide who is to follow the trawler and who is to follow the van. A few of the bald eagles, owls, and black-crowned night heron will follow the van. They are determined to discover where the trawler and van come from and go to.

Mrs. Owl contributes, "My remaining children and I will watch and protect the cove, our Point, and Magnolia Grove."

"Hoot, hoot, hoot," Mrs. Owl calls into the woods. Owls swiftly fly to her side. She counts twelve in all. She is pleased that so many of her family have come to help.

"Children, we will all rest until the skiff makes its appearance. TONIGHT, THE ANIMALS AND HUMANS WORK TOGETHER TO SAVE THE RIVER!"

"Captain is going to be pleased, huh, Momma?"

"Yes, Kitty, you have done well. I am very proud of you, my young one. Be proud of yourself."

"I am not so young. I am all grown up, Momma."

9 ~ LOOMING DANGER

Captain and Sara enjoy the Point, forgetting the looming danger. "It is easy to understand why Kitty loves it here."

K itty and Sara find Captain at the New Dock and working in Betty's engine room. Betty is a combination sailboat and motorboat, a beautiful Nordhavn 56' motorsailer.

Being the perfect liveaboard luxury trawler, Captain makes many long journeys aboard Betty.

Sara has also traveled with Captain since she was very young. When at sea, they always set aside personal time for fun and adventure.

Captain often says he can always count on the unexpected at sea. After all, the sea is very unpredictable. Therefore, when at sea, Sara has learned to stay safe inside Betty. She loves sitting at the helm with Captain as they sail and motor over the open waters.

When docked on land, and when water is calm, Sara will go outside on the aft deck. There she suns in a protective hole that opens from the pilothouse. Captain's number one safety priority at sea has always been Sara.

~

This past spring, Captain and Sara sailed Betty to the tip of the Florida Keys. After that, they crossed the Straits of Florida to the Yucatan Peninsula into Mexico.

On the Yucatan, Captain docked at a beautiful spot south of Cancun called the Marina El Cid. At the Marina El Cid, Sara surprised Captain with the birth of her son, one amazing and rare male calico. When Sara heard Captain say, "What a beautiful kitty," she liked the name so much, she decided to name her son Kitty.

With his new family addition, worried and attentive Captain stayed at Marina El Cid a little longer than planned. He was determined he and Betty were not moving anywhere until Sara and Kitty were strong and ready for travel. He chose to stay near veterinarians and stores for any need, large or small, that his best friend or her son might have. Only one in 3,000 Calicos are born male. Kitty is special!

So, on that work trip, Captain had to quickly rearrange his schedule. He ended up being a few days late for some very important consulting appointments at several important schools and research facilities along the shores of the Gulf of Mexico.

~

But now, both Sara and Kitty will get to travel with Captain on Betty. Kitty shares a stateroom with Momma, but they both mostly stay in Captain's quarters.

The smallest stateroom, next to Captain, belongs to Rod. For years, on weekends, holidays, and in summer, Rod comes to enjoy Magnolia Grove and sail with Captain.

Rod is very important to Kitty. He became Kitty's best human friend the very first time they met. Betty, Captain, and Kitty picked up Rod in the Florida Keys on their return from Mexico. Grace allowed Rod to take some time off after graduating from high school to go sailing. He then dropped his sailboat, Little Puppy, off in the Keys for a total refit.

Aboard Betty, Kitty and Rod have shared many adventures.

Over the years, Captain often gets Rod home to Maryland late and barely in time for school to start. This summer was no different.

So, when Rod and Captain were late, Grace was, to say the least, a little mad at her brother. Rod almost missed his important first day of college. And Captain almost missed the honor of giving the opening ceremony speech at the very prestigious United States Naval Academy in Annapolis. The academy has been training U.S. Navy and Marine Corps officers since 1845.

Nonetheless, Grace cannot argue the positive influence her brother has on her son. Rod is fortunate to attend the United States Naval Academy, just as her brother, Sam, did.

Bad news at Hidden Cove

Captain tries to listen. Sara and Kitty are both speaking at the same time trying to explain the successful results of the Great Gathering. All the animals are on board to help.

Kitty starts talking about the little fox chasing the rabbit.

"Can you two possibly speak one at a time, please? I cannot understand one word either of you are saying!"

After many questions, all becomes clear to Captain. "Mr. and Mrs. Owl and the other animals really understood and are going to help? This is great news!" Captain is pleased.

"I am going to find Rod now, Momma." Kitty proclaims. "We will meet you later on Betty."

He looks his mother in the eye. "I want you to be very careful, Momma. Those varmints are very dangerous. So is that poison they are moving."

Her voice softens as she looks at her son behaving so grown. "I should be telling you to be careful, Kitty. You listen to Rod tonight and stay very close to him."

"I will, Momma. See you later!"

Next door, Kitty finds Rod checking his list and loading his truck. Rod looks up, very happy to see his friend. "There you are. I packed us both some snacks, but you had better eat dinner before we leave, Kitty. We do not need your stomach to start growling and you begging for food while we are gathering evidence."

Kitty understands the word, "dinner" and decides it is a great idea. He gallops to the food and water bowls that Miss Grace keeps in her kitchen.

With the sun set, Rod and Kitty drive to the other side of the Severn River. They reach the area directly across from Kitty Point and turn onto a dirt lane that leads to Hidden Cove.

Rod talks a little to Kitty but mostly to himself. "I drove over here earlier and found this dirt road to Hidden Cove. We will drive to the end and circle around. I will show you what those criminals have done. I took photos, too, but it is not safe to get out and walk around on the circle. You will see."

"Yes" is all Kitty can say to Rod, but to himself he thinks, *I think I will stay here in Rod's lap. Hidden Cove is not safe!*

Kitty sits on Rod's lap with his front paws pressed on the side door glass. The truck reaches the end of Hidden Cove's dirt road. There is an opening big enough for the truck to circle around.

Kitty gasps in alarm. The headlights reveal dead vegetation and dying trees along the edge of the turn-around.

"No! No! No!" Kitty yells. He then buries his head in Rod's chest. Kitty knows how very important trees and plants are to the animals. He has learned to love all life. Kitty's eyes fill with tears.

Rod pulls Kitty close. "Come here, Kitty. I know it is bad. Do not look any more. Everything will be OK. Captain knows what to do. We will fix everything."

With darkness, Rod feels the cooler temperature and notes the beginning of fall. As he drives away, headlights once again reveal the horror at Hidden Cove. He hugs Kitty tighter. "We will fix everything."

"Yes, yes!" Kitty cries.

Rod does not realize that "we" includes a small group of bald eagles, owls, and black-crowned night heron safely sitting high in the trees on the other side of Hidden Cove. Tonight, the great birds are here to help. They hope to find out where the human varmints haul that poison.

Rod circles the truck around and drives only a short distance towards the road before stopping. He quickly backs his truck onto a very narrow lane overgrown with brush. Rod parks his truck on a bend in the lane. The location offers good protection. The truck goes dark.

"No one has used this for a long time. Once it joined the circle we just drove around, but now it has too many bushes and trees growing on it for use. Hiding among this thick brush, we will be safe to listen and collect evidence."

"Evidence!" Kitty repeats clearly, "Evidence!"

"What a big word evidence is, Kitty! Good boy!"

Suddenly, Kitty is up on the dashboard. His ears perk up as he points towards the lane.

It takes a few more seconds, but soon Rod hears the van, too. The van's windows must be open, for Kitty and Rod clearly hear men inside fussing at each other.

"Kitty, you stay in the truck. It is not safe for you to come with me. I am going to get as close as possible, take some pictures, and hopefully gather evidence. I will leave the windows open a few inches for you; I will be back soon." Rod disappears around the bend.

Safely hiding behind the thick brush, Rod can clearly hear the two men inside the van talking. "Tomorrow night is our last trip here. Come Monday, we move to our new location." Rod snaps photos with the night binoculars.

Rod hears this pending change in schedule and whispers to himself, "We are running out of time to catch those varmints!"

"Yes, yes!" Kitty says quietly.

In disbelief, Rod looks down at Kitty standing beside him in full attention and on guard.

"Oh, no, Kitty, what are you doing here? I told you to stay in the truck." Rod picks Kitty up and holds him close. "How did you get out of the truck anyway? You could get yourself and me into big trouble being out here, Kitty. I am certain you know better."

Kitty responds in a very low but stern cat voice. "Meow, it is too dangerous for you to be out here by yourself, Rod. Meow! Miss Grace would never approve, meow!"

Rod cannot understand all of Kitty's cat chatter, but he knows Kitty is scolding him. He realizes he has no choice but to let Kitty stay with him. He zips Kitty inside his jacket, and Rod continues to take photos for evidence.

"Meow, Rod, meow! You really need to be looked after, meow!"

"Stop that meowing, Kitty!"

Kitty hears the familiar sound of the coming skiff. He looks over at Rod, but he does not seem to notice it yet. *Rod sure cannot hear very well either.*

"Grr," Kitty growls. "Grr."

The skiff backs up, docks, and two men stand and stretch. *Yep. It is the man with the black hat and the man with the long, full beard! They are the same human varmints that live next door to Miss Brown!*

"Grr. Grr."

"Shush, Kitty. You will get us in trouble."

Two men wearing black rubber suits get out of the van. They carefully put on gloves and face masks. The masked men open the back of the large van and begin to carry crates to the pier.

One masked man says to the other, "This is a big load tonight. The boss will be pleased. Be careful transferring these crates onto the skiff. Some of them are leaking. You know this stuff can really hurt us."

From the skiff, the tall man in the black hat overhears the masked men. "Hurt us, you say? Did you say these crates could hurt us?"

One masked man replies. "Yes, toxic chemicals can kill."

The man in the black hat now sounds angry. "That company lied to us! They told us to keep quiet about this job because they did not want their competition knowing their business. Nobody said anything about toxic chemicals or any risk of getting hurt."

One masked man responds. "You mean to tell me that you cannot tell this stuff is toxic? Why else would we wear this black protective gear?"

The man in the black hat feels foolish, but honestly replies. "We figured you might not want to be seen."

One of the masked men laugh. "Are you two ignorant or just stupid?"

The man in the black hat answered in a loud and strong voice. "We must be ignorant. We do not have much of an education. But the way I hear it, you already know this stuff is dangerous. You even wear black protective clothes. And yet, here you both are, still working. So, you tell us, who is stupid?"

The four men finish in cold silence. The two men with the black protective clothing return to their van, remove their clothing, and drive away.

At Hidden Cove's old pier, the now very cautious tall man with the black hat and the man with the long, full beard board their skiff. Both avoid touching their cargo.

The man in the black hat scratches his head. "We knew the money was too good, Barney. Why didn't we listen to ourselves? That company we have been working for is crooked! We must get this stuff off our boat!"

The heavily loaded skiff travels slower than usual. It shoots off its flare to notify the trawler they are on their way. The boat clears the mouth of Hidden Cove and makes its way across the river in the direction of Kitty Point.

The men in the skiff stare forward in deep thought. They know this company they found work with cares nothing for them. It has used them, risking their lives by exposing them to leaky chemicals.

The tall man in the black hat speaks first. "The company could have killed us, Barney. If we had any chemical spills in the skiff, it could have killed anyone that boarded. Of all things! We take kids fishing in this skiff! Let's get rid of these crates, collect our pay tomorrow, and never return."

Barney pulls on his beard, as if stroking it helps him think. Maybe it does. He has little use for words and seldom speaks, but this time he has found need. He is very serious and absolute with his tone. "Abe, after we unload, we are going to completely clean this boat and forget that company and the money they owe us."

"Yes, OK Barney, I agree. Now that we know about the danger, we won't be back!"

Abe in his black hat and Barney with the long, full beard silently steer to meet the trawler one last time.

Still hidden in the brush, Rod and Kitty hear the van's engine start. They rush to get back to Rod's truck.

"We must hurry to follow them, Kitty. It may be too late."

"Hold on Kitty. Hold on. Stay in there!" Rod holds one arm over Kitty to protect him inside his jacket. He uses the other arm to push back tree limbs as his jeans tear through brush and briar. They can hear a horn honking.

Rod and Kitty finally make it to the truck. Rod slides into the seat and unzips his jacket. He pants and whispers. "The van does not know we are here, so what are they honking at?"

Kitty jumps onto Rod's lap and peers out the window. *Oh, the Buck family is here and standing in the middle of the road!*

A large young buck stands in front of Rod's truck. It stands firmly and blocks their exit.

"Oh, no. This is not a good time for the deer to block the road. Kitty, it is holding us in place. We will have to wait."

A few seconds later, they hear the van drive by, still blowing its horn. The buck blocking Rod's truck slowly steps aside.

Rod laughs and uses the light of the moon to guide his truck. Several bucks line the edge of the dirt road. They formally nod greetings and direct Rod and Kitty safely forward.

"Those deer saved us by being in the middle of the road. They slowed down that van so we can follow."

"Help, help!" yells Kitty.

Rod clearly hears Kitty yell the word help.

He asks, "Help with what Kitty? If it is the dark, we will turn on the headlights when we get to the hard-surfaced road."

Rod does not understand that Kitty is explaining that Mr. Owl had sent the Buck family to help, too.

The van goes around a curve and Rod turns on his headlights. He attempts to be just another vehicle on the road.

Rod does not see the bald eagles, the owls, and the black-crowned night herons following high above the van. However, Kitty does.

The van goes several miles and slows down in front of a large, fenced yard. Someone is waiting with the gates open. As soon as the van enters, the same person closes the gates.

"I did not see this bad luck coming." Rod reports to Kitty.

Once again, Rod does not see the bald eagles, the owls, and the black-crowned night herons fly over the fence to continue following the van. Thank goodness, Kitty does.

"Meow." Trying to tell Rod about the birds helping, Kitty looks at Rod, up at the birds, and then back to Rod.

"What is it, Kitty? What do you see?" Rod looks up. "Are those birds?"

"Yes, yes!" Kitty proclaims.

Rod does not understand the significance of the birds flying above the truck this night.

That is a lot of help in the sky, Kitty notes.

Just after the gate, Rod drives onto an open lot where other vehicles park. They sit in the dark waiting to see the van again.

Rod leans forward. "Finally, some movement!"

Rod and Kitty see lights move through the fenced yard and disappear behind a row of trucks.

Without warning, headlights of a vehicle shine and travel away from the other side of the yard. It speeds down a road, around a curve, and disappears through the woods.

Rod yells. "They left from the other side of the storage yard! There must be a gate on the other side to escape! They are too far ahead now. We have lost them, Kitty."

Kitty watches the birds follow the van. They disappear behind the woods.

With the varmints in the van being so far ahead of them now, Rod and Kitty have no choice but to drive back home to Magnolia Grove.

Rod speaks loudly. "We will try to join Captain and Betty at Kitty Point. They might have to shove off and attempt to follow the trawler into the Mobjack Bay."

"Rod," Kitty clearly yells, "Go! Go!" *We must hurry and not miss Betty. Captain and Momma need us.*

Meanwhile at Kitty Point

The night sky and scattered trees edging Kitty Point may be just enough cover to keep the varmint trawler from seeing Betty. Captain has her tucked as far back in East Cove as the water depth will allow. The bottom of Betty is almost touching the cove's bottom, but Captain knows that the rising tide will keep her safe and out of the silt.

Captain and Sara stand at the end of Kitty Point. Earlier, they used Betty's 10-foot dinghy to cross the shallow water. They had come ashore for an excellent view of the river.

For a moment, they both enjoy the night and forget about the looming danger. Captain catches the silhouette of Hidden Cove across the river.

"It is easy to understand why Kitty loves it here, Sara. It is private and beautiful with peaceful views of the Severn River and out onto the Mobjack Bay."

Sara agrees. "No wonder Kitty comes out here at night. It must be quite an adventure for him."

"Yes, this is an adventure by itself, Sara. I have only visited Kitty Point a few times by boat to clean the shoreline. I have purposely left Kitty Point, its marsh, and the East Cove to nature and the local animals."

Across the river, Captain and Sara see a flare rise in the sky. It shoots out sparks and falls into the river just outside the mouth of Hidden Cove.

"Just as Kitty described it, Captain! Now the trawler and skiff will meet in the river." Sara sits tall, guarding her Captain.

In the moonlight, Captain cannot help but notice the resemblance of Sara to Kitty. They have the same profile and stance.

"Look, Sara, Hidden Cove cannot be seen by anyone upriver. No wonder those criminals can hide so easily to do their harm.

I wonder if Rod and Kitty will be here soon. Sara, we must follow the trawler tonight with or without the boys."

Mr. and Mrs. Owl watch and listen from their favorite tree limb. They wait for the skiff and trawler to return. They also wait for the birds that are following the van to return with news. They all hear Rod's truck arrive and park at Magnolia Grove.

Rod and Kitty race across the front yard towards the woods. Without slowing down, Kitty enters the thin path that cuts through the woods to Kitty Point. Rod tries to follow.

"Go, go!" Kitty yells as he leads Rod through the woods. The path is narrow and low. It slows Rod down. He slips further behind.

Kitty hears the small engine of Betty's dinghy start as he reaches the Point's clearing. Captain and Sara are ready to shove off and head back to Betty. Kitty runs as fast as he can.

I must stop them before they leave us behind. "Meow, Momma! Momma! Stop! Meow!" He yells as he runs.

Sara gets very excited. "Captain, I hear Kitty!"

"Meow, meow, and here I am! Here I am!" Kitty keeps running to the water's edge. Without thinking, he leaps with all his might and jumps farther than he has ever jumped. Kitty's belly slides across the forward deck. He then tumbles headfirst into the dinghy.

Sara rushes to her son. "Oh Kitty, that was a dangerous jump. You could have been hurt!"

"Meow, I am OK, Momma; Rod is behind me and trying to catch up!"

On top of worrying about Rod, now Kitty and Sara hear the fishing trawler in the Severn River. They know time is running out, and the trawler will soon meet the skiff in front of Kitty Point and transfer the poison.

"Meow, here come the varmint boats. You better tell Captain, Momma. You know he cannot hear very well."

Sara quickly tells Captain about the boats coming, but he ignores her. He has already turned around. Captain knows when Rod is home, Kitty is seldom far behind him. In this case, Kitty must be ahead of Rod.

Much to Captain's relief, when the dinghy hits the shore, Rod clears the forest and makes his way into the moonlight. He reaches the dinghy and whispers loudly as possible.

"Permission to come aboard, Captain." He gasps for breath while pulling twigs and briars out of his hair and off his clothing.

"Permission gladly granted," whispers a smiling Captain. "We sure are grateful you two made it, but we must hurry. Fill us in on the details when we are comfortably aboard Betty."

With Captain's crew fully intact, the dinghy once again points towards Betty. It crosses over the shallow waters to the center of the cove where Betty safely waits.

They all hear the fishing trawler closing in on Kitty Point.

It is too late to hoist the dinghy back onto the top of the pilot house. The noise would give them away. So, Captain anchors the dinghy in the cove, and the four of them quietly sneak up Betty's swim platform.

"Good," smiles Captain. "We have moored Betty far enough back into East Cove for the trees to hide us from the trawler and skiff."

With all four safely in the pilothouse and saloon, Kitty and Momma stand guard and listen through the open screened windows. They can hear much better than Rod or Captain.

Rod whispers to Captain. "It is bad at Hidden Cove, Captain. The area around the dock is void of life. I do not know how, but the two men on the skiff did not realize they were moving dangerous poison. When they found out, they became angry with the men that arrived in the van. Also, there is more bad news. On Monday, the operation moves to a new location."

"There is no time to waste." Captain is very concerned. "These criminals must be caught! In addition, a professional environmental cleanup will be needed at Hidden Cove."

Kitty has not taken his eyes off the trawler. "Momma, they are the same men I saw the first night. See? There is the short stocky man and the wild white-haired man. The white-haired man is loud and mean, Momma. I think he is their captain."

Rod and Captain hear and see the two men's features as they light and then relight their cigars. Rod whispers, "I do not know them, Captain."

"Me neither." Captain agrees.

A slight breeze blows through the port screens.

"The skiff is almost here, Momma."

"I hear it, Kitty. I hear it."

The skiff with its heavy crates, reaches the trawler and ties alongside it with ropes. The stocky man on the trawler and the two men on the skiff begin transporting crates onto the trawler.

Abe and Barney have buttoned up their jackets, trying to be careful to touch the crates as little as possible. The stocky man from the trawler speaks down to the men in the skiff. "Why are you two so slow tonight?"

Abe offers a cold look up at the trawler. Loudly, he replies, "We are just being extra careful. You don't want any of this stuff to leak onto your boat or into the river, do you?"

The wind helps carry their voices to Betty's crew. They all hear what comes next.

The man on the trawler with the wild white hair looks over at the skiff. His voice sounds angry. "First, this trawler is not mine, so I do not care what gets into it. Second, if I had my way, these crates would have been in the river all along. But I am paid to deliver the crates to a ship waiting in open water."

Captain and Rod gasp realizing how bad the men in the trawler are. Kitty was correct from the beginning. Captain tells Rod, "These varmints are like no others ever seen in this area."

"Now hurry up, Abe and Barney!" barks the captain of the trawler.

Abe adjusts his black hat and barks back. "Move the crates yourself if you do not like the speed that we are doing it. These crates are dangerous. They could have killed us, and you did not even bother to warn us."

"Quit whining. You are paid plenty well," argues the varmint trawler captain.

With the last crate loaded, the wild haired captain on the trawler calls out to the skiff. "Barney, board the trawler, so we can get out of here and finish."

Quiet Barney is now the one staring up at the two men in the trawler. "Money will do us no good if we are dead. I won't be coming along to help you tonight."

The wild white-haired captain looks at Abe. "Don't ask me to go," Abe yells. "I stay with my boat. Let's go Barney!"

"The boss is not going to like this," barks the wild white-haired captain from the trawler.

With the last crate loaded, Abe and Barney abruptly turn the skiff upriver and head towards Browns Bay. They never look back. Barney and Abe have no interest in seeing that fishing trawler or hearing from its company again.

.

"What is that Owl dropping?

With a new load of dangerous and illegal crates, the varmint trawler steers into the night towards the Mobjack Bay. The boat's captain grunts as if in pain. He is upset that the man with the long, full beard is not helping unload the boat tonight. He will have to handle the crates himself because tonight, he only has one other crew member. Barney, flatly refusing to help, takes off on the skiff with Abe, the man in the black hat.

Suddenly, and quite unfortunately for the trawler's captain, an explosive and banging sound comes from the engine. The captain quickly attempts to turn the wheel. He cannot afford the trawler breaking down in Mobjack Bay's open water. They need to reach a safe place to hide somewhere on the Severn River.

As the trawler makes its eruptive sound, Abe and Barney are already steering into Brown's Cove.

"Barney, do you hear that awful noise?"

"Yeah, Abe. It sounds like that captain ran his trawler so hard the engine blew up and exploded. It is trying to come this way!"

"Barney, we need to hurry. If that boat passes Browns Bay, those men might recognize us under these lights. They might seek our help. We want nothing to do with their problems."

"Agreed!" Barney grabs the bow line and readies to tie at Brown's dock. They cut the lights and decide to clean the skiff in the morning.

Everyone aboard Betty also hears the horrible noises. Kitty paces back and forth along the porthole's ledge. "Momma, that varmint boat is in big trouble. We have it trapped upriver! Tell Captain we need to know where it goes, Momma. We really do!"

As if Captain understood and commanded Mother Nature herself to blow in and help, up comes a sudden wind. Captain smiles with his turn of luck. He orders Rod to raise Betty's sails and then heads her quietly out of the cove and onto the river.

Captain knows his decision is a bit risky. "Hopefully, that crippled trawler will be too busy to notice us from behind."

They ease Betty out of East Cove and turn upriver. "Yes, yes!" Kitty leans into the port. *We are coming after you!*

The westerly wind assists the crippled trawler up the river. It pushes dangerously close to Magnolia Grove's shore.

The short and stocky crew member stands at the cabin door and reports. "We better stay away from that long pier on the starboard side. That big house has too many lights." The trawler limps past the cove where Magnolia Grove's pier extends.

Suddenly, the trawler's engine sputters more, clanks, and completely stops. The wild white-haired captain attempting to steer calls back, "If we are not careful, we will run ashore in that sandbar ahead. Be ready to push off the shoals… now!"

The stocky man uses a telescoping boat hook and pushes to clear the shoals, but he fails. The trawler suddenly runs aground.

Distracted by their own bad situation, the varmints have no time to notice that behind their stern, Captain and Rod skillfully and quietly tie Betty to the end of the New Dock.

Nor do they notice members of the Owl family following.

The men on the varmint boat begin to panic and plead with the river to free them from their prison of sand and silt.

Eventually, their pleas seem answered. The nudge from the rising tide and the bounce from the waves finally free their boat. Once again, the varmint trawler continues drifting northwest along the Severn River's shore.

The stocky man on the trawler squeals in delight. "Look! We are drifting into a wooded cove with a pier. Luck is with us!" The crew head towards the Old Dock, a spot they believe to be safe to hide.

At the end of the New Dock, Kitty, Sara, Rod, and Captain observe the grounded trawler being set free. Kitty, very agitated, yells, "Look Momma! That boat is drifting to our Old Dock! Do you see? You better tell Captain! This is bad, Momma. Oh no, they are going to poison our water, Momma!"

Worried herself, Sara tries to comfort her son. "Calm down, Kitty. Captain will know what to do."

Captain enters the saloon and dials his friend. "I know it is very late, Mark, but I think you will want to hear this update."

Rod patiently waits, and Captain hangs up. "Well, Captain?"

"Well, Mark seems delighted with the news; but for our own safety, he cautions us to stay away from the criminals and wait for the authorities."

"But we will watch them anyway, won't we, Captain?"

"I think we will, Rod. I think we will."

The poison loaded trawler drifts close enough to the Old Dock for the crew to lasso its pilings. They all sigh in relief, being pleased with their bit of presumed luck.

The stocky crew member pokes his head into the cabin. "Captain, there are too many birds gathered in the trees."

"Never mind those birds," replies the gruff captain. "They are the least of our worries. We need to get this trawler ready for an innocent looking tow out of here! Our tow needs to be here well before twilight because this river will be busy in the morning with early traffic."

Meanwhile, the crew does not notice the many more birds arriving in the trees.

The bald eagles, the owls, and the black-crowned night herons return from following Rod and the van. They quietly land high in the trees.

The lead eagle flies over and reports to Mr. Owl. "We followed the van to a large barn on a farm far southwest from Magnolia Grove. The men left the van in the barn and left the farm from a different truck. There were other vehicles there, too. At least we know where they store the poison. And that smell is everywhere!"

Mr. Owl nods his head in approval. "Mr. Eagle, you have done well discovering where the poison is kept. Your team has helped save us from a terrible fate."

The birds, now taking serious guard over the waters at the Old Dock, hear a truck turn onto Magnolia Drive.

Creeping along with its lights off, the truck mysteriously drives up and parks just before reaching Magnolia Cottage.

A man quietly gets out of the truck and carefully looks around. He feels the winds warning of an approaching storm. Working his way to the edge of the trees near the Old Dock, he proceeds to quietly spy on the stranded trawler.

Meanwhile, Betty's crew disembarks. "Meow! Rod, we must go! Those varmints are going to poison the water. Meow!"

Kitty worries about the water and land around the Old Dock. He worries about his friends and family. *We must hurry.*

Rod, not understanding Kitty's pleas, reaches down and pets him. "Kitty, what are you going on about? Are you worried about those men? Be patient. We will be catching those varmints soon enough."

Kitty forgets everything except the dangerous boat at the Old Dock. In a burst of impatience, and running as fast as he can, Kitty leaves everyone behind. *I need to keep an eye on those varmints. I must protect everyone at Magnolia Grove!*

Kitty cuts behind the Boat Barn to the Old Dock. He avoids the man spying from under the trees. Kitty quietly runs across the lane to Mr. and Mrs. Max's waterfront treehouse by the Old Dock.

The clanging trawler has already woken the squirrel family. They hide inside their treehouse while Max investigates.

By luck, Kitty and Max meet at the bottom of the tree. "Max, what is Ronnie Brown doing here? Does he see us?"

"Nah. Humans can't see good. His truck is under a tree by the house, and he has been spying around here for a while.

Kid, we got big trouble. That trawler at the Old Dock has the same stinking smell as the skiff we discovered in that boathouse."

"Yes, Max. It is the same smell and the same varmint trawler. And it is full of poisonous crates, too!"

"I somehow knew that, Kid. Also, that clanking noise woke up the Mrs. She is none too happy about it, either. If she knows you are here, Kid, everything is going to be your stinking fault."

Kitty knows what Max says is very true. The Mrs. really does not like nor trust Kitty. *I must worry about that later. For now, I must protect Mrs. Max and all of Magnolia Grove.*

The varmint trawler's captain is on the phone again. "I understand. Call right away if rescue pushes too close to sunrise. We will dump this stuff here and escape with an innocent sunrise tow." He laughs, and Kitty's hair stands on end.

Dump this stuff… dump… "Max, I think those varmints are going to dump those crates of poison in the water. They might get away before we catch them. We have real bad trouble, Max. Oh, where is Captain and Rod? And to add to trouble, that storm is fast approaching."

The wind blows harder, the river swells, and the water around the Old Dock becomes very choppy. The roaring sounds prevent Ronnie Brown, still hiding under the trees, from hearing anything. He does notice an unusual number of birds gathering high in the trees.

Max stands tall. His ears twitch. "Hear that boat, Kid?"

"Yes, Max. Is it coming here?"

"I bet it is coming to rescue that stinking busted trawler."

"Max, the rain is coming, and so is that rescue boat. I must find out what is going on. Keep an eye on everything, Max."

"Kid!"

Before Max objects, Kitty races to the end of the dock. He hides behind one of the pilings and watches as the boat rocks back and forth. The crew struggles to stay on their feet.

Kitty sees the masthead light of an approaching boat. *Is that the rescue boat? It must be. What else could it be?*

This storm is so noisy. What are those varmints doing? By now they must know about the boat coming to rescue them.

Lightning splits open the sky, and rain fiercely pounds the ground. Max quickly darts up to the safety of his tree den.

Inside, his family is dry and finally asleep. He peers out into the storm. "I sure hope the Kid is OK."

As the rescue boat gets closer, Kitty sees it is a twin to the nightly varmint boat loaded with poisons. *If there are two varmint boats, I fear there may be more! I must investigate. Oh, where is everyone? Captain and Momma would know what to do. They always know what to do.*

Kitty sees the wild white-haired captain come out of his cabin. He ends his cell phone call with a big smile and laughter. "Get ready for tow. We are out of here!"

The rescue boat comes into sight. Wasting no time, it positions itself to tow the broken and poison carrying trawler.

I must do something!

Probably not being his best choice, Kitty runs towards the varmint boat. With all his might, he leaps into the air, trying to soar like a flying squirrel over the water. Kitty lands, digging in his claws as he slides across the stern. He is grateful when a coil of rope stops him.

Kitty hides and peaks above the rope pile. He looks and listens. He worries not for himself. He worries for all of Magnolia Grove.

Kitty, now on the poison-filled trawler, hides and heads towards open water.

Where are these boats going?

Ronnie Brown no longer hides under the trees near the Old Dock. He runs onto the dock just as the two trawlers pull away. He angrily looks out into the dark, rainy night.

Mrs. Owl turns her head from back to front and drops from her perch. Swooping through the trees, she squawks out orders, flies out onto the river, and disappears into the night.

Mr. Owl lands in the tree his mate just left. Frantically he looks around and loudly demands, "Where is Mother?"

The many birds report that Mrs. Owl has ordered all the birds to help stop the dangerous trawlers from escaping.

"Mother always knows best." Mr. Owl immediately leads his entire flock of birds over the river and into the rainy night.

The rain pounds as Captain and Sara stop at Magnolia Cottage to pick up Rod. Rain pours off Captain, but Sara is dry and tucked inside his long raincoat. She peeks out at Rod.

Rod is ready to go. "Captain, where is Kitty?"

Captain looks alarmed. "We thought he was with you!" Sara stretches her head out and looks around.

"Kitty is not here, Sara, but I think I know where he is." Rod covers his head and runs.

Rod is pacing the shore in worry by the time Captain and Sara come upon Ronnie Brown standing on the Old Dock.

"Ronnie Brown!" Captain calls. "Ronnie Brown!" Ronnie appears to be in shock.

Captain suddenly realizes what happened and shouts, "The trawler is gone! We were watching it on my security monitors less than five minutes ago!"

Ronnie finally speaks. "Well, we have more worry. The Virginia Marine Police and the Coast Guard are about to enter the Mobjack Bay. They are still about 15 minutes out.

I needed to stall those criminal trawlers; but it is too late now. I am not to interfere until help arrives. We cannot risk that crew dumping their poison in our waters tonight."

Things finally click into place and Captain laughs aloud, "Oh, I understand now! You are with the authorities and have been working undercover! It is very nice to meet the real Ronnie Brown!

Do not fear a loss yet, Ronnie Brown. Much help is coming. Those varmints will not escape. We have our own network of spies here at Magnolia Grove!"

Ronnie Brown looks around. "Well, Captain, the only network I see tonight is a large number of birds in the rain."

This time Captain chuckles to himself.

It is so dark that Captain nor Ronnie notice Rod pacing the shores along the Old Dock, muttering, "Oh no! Kitty is aboard that trawler! I just know he is!"

Fight for freedom

Indeed, Kitty is aboard the varmint trawler with the poison crates. The rain drenches his fur. He clings to the coiled rope, trying to see and listen. The rain pounds and the boat rocks.

Kitty is about to jump down into the hull of the varmint boat for safety when the trawler rocks even more violently. The coiled rope begins to unravel from the rain's gushing water.

Kitty rolls over the rope and slides across the bow. Desperate, he attempts to grab hold of the deck with all his claws.

Kitty spins around, and his back half goes over the edge. Frightened, he hangs on to the lip with all his might and tries to pull himself up. He looks down. *Oh, no. Momma says I can swim, but those waves are too big. I will never make it to shore.* He pulls up again. He almost makes it over the lip. Three paws are secure. The trawler bounces fiercely, and Kitty almost falls again. He feels himself getting weaker.

"Help! Help!" he screams. When the boat bounces once again, Kitty loses his grip and falls towards the black water.

Fear sets in. *I must swim!*

Kitty braces himself to hit the water, knowing he most likely will never make it alive through the rough waves. "Help, help!" Kitty screams a last desperate plea for help as his paws feel the wet, cold water.

Gravity forces Kitty's frightening plunge into the river. As soon as he goes underwater, Kitty desperately begins to swim up. The water is so rough. *I can't hold my breath much longer!* He swims harder. Suddenly, his head rises above the water. Kitty gasps for a precious and life-saving breath.

Kitty aimlessly swims with all his might. His only thought is to keep his head above the waves. "Help! Help!" He once again yells. Another wave splashes over his head. Kitty is very weak. He swallows much sea water and begins to cough.

Suddenly, something grabs Kitty by his shoulders. He begins to rise out of the water. Kitty panics and instinctively fights for freedom.

"No! No!" Kitty screams.

Struggling with all his remaining energy, Kitty suddenly feels intense pain as the grip on his shoulders tighten. As he continues to rise above the water and into the night, Kitty hears a soothing voice.

"Calm yourself Master Kitty, or my claws will hurt you!"

Is that Mrs. Owl's voice? "Mrs. Owl?"

"You are safe, Master Kitty. You are safe. You have not been out of my sight. We will talk about this later. For now, please relax. You are a bit heavy with so much water weight."

Kitty suddenly yells, "Varmints! We must stop the varmints!"

"Master Kitty, do not worry. Papa and I are taking care of your varmints."

Mrs. Owl turns towards Magnolia Grove. Within a minute, she flies by Papa and his flock of birds heading towards the trawlers. The couple is very pleased to see each other. Mr. Owl is even pleased to see that Kitty is safe.

Mr. Owl and the relentless birds keep flying through the torrential storm. The wind and rain do not slow them.

Soon, the mob of birds spots the varmint trawlers. Mr. Owl dives towards the boats to gain a clearer position.

"Attack right!" he orders the right flank of birds. Mr. Owl lands on the radar antenna to observe and lead the battle.

A group of birds breaks off from the flock and swarm down upon the rear trawler. The crew panics. There is no time for defense, but they do manage to run inside the cabin. The birds land everywhere on the trawler except on the poison crates. They pound on the decks and hit the windows. The crew shakes in fear. They only see and hear angry, vicious birds.

The captain of the lead rescue trawler comes out of his cabin and looks behind. He whispers, "What is that men? Are those birds?"

Next, the second flank attacks. They swoop over the lead trawler, instilling terror upon its crew. So many birds land at once that the crew cannot make it to the safety of their cabin. Together, they dive under the stern and hide within its storage.

As the birds all work together, both crews dare not move. The lead rescue trawler now steers itself in circles.

Soon, search lights pass over the trawlers. The Coast Guard and Marine Police spot the varmint boats.

What a strange sight for the officials to see so many birds holding in custody two imprisoned criminal boats. They stare in wonder as Mr. Owl circles them and squawks loudly. "I leave this to you, now."

The Coast Guard and Marine Police do not understand Mr. Owl, but they do marvel at the sight of all the birds lifting off the two trawlers at once and flying away. Mr. Owl leads the birds back towards Magnolia Grove.

The Marine Police board the towed trawler, find the toxic waste, and arrest both crews. The Coast Guard further assists by towing both trawlers to the impound yard.

~

The story unfolded when Barney and Abe realized they were transporting illegal dangerous poison. They immediately called their friend, Miss Brown, for help. Miss Brown, in turn, called her brother, Ronnie.

It happens that Ronnie Brown works undercover for Mark Green, who also is Captain's friend. Ronnie's job has been to follow the toxic waste villains these last few weeks. Thus far, the criminals have eluded Mark's team by frequently changing location.

With Miss Brown's help, Barney and Abe told the authorities all they knew and pointed them to the criminals.

Nobody questioned how Captain knew where the farm storing the toxic chemicals was located. They assumed Rod had discovered it.

The birds had followed the van to the farm. The birds then reported to Mr. Owl the location of the stored toxic waste. Later on, Mr. Owl sent word to Captain through Kitty and Sara.

The authorities raid the farm. They collect dangerous evidence and find many criminals at the farm. These additional criminals lead the authorities to a large barge that moors every night in the Mobjack Bay. The illegal barge collects all the toxic chemicals that many varmint trawlers deliver.

The criminal ring collapses, thanks to Abe and Barney calling Miss Brown. Authorities confiscate the barge and arrest its company owners.

~

Flying high

Kitty feels deep gratitude. Mrs. Owl has just saved him. He tries to relax for this new adventure of flying high in the air for the long flight home.

Kitty feels excitement flying in the air. He is safe under the protective wings of Mrs. Owl. He does not mind the pain in his shoulders from her clutch. Nor does he mind the torrential rain beating hard against both Mrs. Owl and him.

Oh, no. I smell blood. Momma is going to be mad at me for letting this happen again. Kitty remembers his previous blood and stitches from when he saved Miss Grace from the coyote attack. *I sure have had a lot of adventures! Adventures can hurt.*

The rain lessens as they get closer to Magnolia Grove. "Things are looking up, Master Kitty. Try to relax another few minutes. We are almost home. I know you are wet and tired."

Rod continues pacing back and forth along the shoreline east of the Old Dock. He does not know what to do. Kitty is missing. The dangerous criminals have escaped. Feeling deep agony, Rod buries his face into his hands. "If something bad happens to Kitty, I will never forgive myself."

Rod hears a "Hoot, hoot!" and "Hoot-a, hoot, hoot!" The sound comes from the river, and it keeps repeating.

"It sounds like one of our Great Horned Owls!" Rod runs to the shore closer to the Old Dock and in the path of the hooting Owl.

Mrs. Owl hoots and hoots as she approaches. She circles Rod, giving Kitty time to yell, "Meow! Rod! It is me! Meow!"

Rod cries in relief and joy, "There you are, Kitty! There you are! I have been so worried!"

After a most beautiful circle pattern, Mrs. Owl gracefully suspends above Rod. She gently drops Kitty into Rod's arms.

For some reason, Rod does not feel a bit odd yelling, "Thank you very much, Owl!"

"Hoot-a, hoot-a, hoot, hoot! I must watch for Papa now." Mrs. Owl flies away.

Mrs. Owl's hooting is so loud, the noise grabs the attention of both Captain and Ronnie Brown on the Old Dock. Ronnie turns to Captain, "I might need glasses, or maybe I need a doctor. I think I just saw an owl drop a live animal into that young man's arms."

Captain feels such relief that he takes a small leap into the air. "That young man is Rod, my nephew. And I believe that Owl just dropped off our very own and special Kitty. As you can see, Kitty also has friends in high places."

Ronnie Brown had not noticed that all along Sara has been peeking out from under Captain's raincoat. He was further surprised when Sara jumps out of Captain's raincoat and quickly runs towards Rod.

Ronnie Brown shakes his head in wonder. "I must have hit my head."

Sara circles Rod's feet. "Kitty! Kitty!" She cries. "My son! Are you hurt?"

Sara pleads, "Rod! Would someone please speak to me?"

Rod finally hears Sara. "I have him, Sara! Kitty is safe! However, I think he is hurt."

"We have you, now, Kitty. You are safe. You are so wet, and you are bleeding at both shoulders. Oh, Kitty, you look so weak. You must have found real trouble this time." Realizing the seriousness of Kitty's condition, Rod and Sara begin to run.

Kitty tries to explain. "Meow! It was so scary, Momma! Meow! I fell off the boat. Then I went under the water. Meow! Rod, I could not breath for a long time, but I finally came up, meow! I was so tired trying to swim. I thought I would drown. Mrs. Owl saved me! Meow! I want my food bowl, meow!"

"Sara, he wants food. He will be OK. Let us get Kitty to the hospital." He smiles for Sara's sake, but Rod is very worried about his bleeding friend.

So, hours before sunrise, Kitty, Rod, and Sara meet Doctor Sue at her animal care hospital. She is none too happy with Kitty's condition, either. She quickly gives Kitty fluids and takes X-rays.

She then cleans Kitty's wounds. "Kitty, these wounds are deep. It looks like something tore you apart. And you have only just healed from your last stitches!" Doctor Sue proceeds to sew six more stitches into Kitty, three in the right shoulder and three in the left.

"OK, that should do it. Kitty, I am convinced you look for trouble!"

"Meow, meow." Sara agrees.

Kitty pouts. "Meow. I am sorry. Meow."

Doctor Sue continues. "Rod, I do not want Kitty going outside for at least two days."

Finally at home, Sara and Rod tuck Kitty into bed and say goodnight. "Meow." Kitty is very tired from his adventure and stitches.

Kitty does not wake up until the next day. He eats a good meal and falls back to sleep. His mother stays by his side, keeping close watch over her son. Then Kitty has no trouble sleeping through the night once again. He dreams of flying through the sky to safety with Mrs. Owl.

Alliances

The second day after Kitty gets home, Kitty and Sara are resting on the porch. Kitty feels so good with his first sunshine since the stitches.

Max comes from behind a bush and joins them. "Hey Kid. I did not think you would ever come out of that stinking house. How are you feeling? We have been a little worried, you know."

"Thank you, Max. My stitches hurt a little, but I am OK."

Mr. and Mrs. Owl quietly land in the tree beside the porch.

"There you are." Mrs. Owl swoops to the ground to get a closer look at Kitty. "Let me look at you, Master Kitty. I have been concerned about how badly I hurt you."

Kitty sits up straight, trying to be brave, but Mrs. Owl can see much pain in his face. "Ah, it's just a few stitches, Mrs. Owl. You did not mean to hurt me. You saved my life!"

Sara greets the Owls. "Kitty explained how frightened he was when you pulled him out of the river. He said he fought you as hard as he could. Thank goodness you won the fight, Mrs. Owl."

"I always do, Miss Sara. Well, sometimes I do let Papa win." They all smile. "But I am so sorry to see those bandages on Master Kitty."

"Mrs. Owl, if you were not on that river, Kitty's fate would be much worse than a few stitches. I owe you a great debt of gratitude. You and your husband are our friends, our allies, forever."

Kitty hangs his head just a little. "I am sorry, Momma. I am sorry, Mrs. Owl. I did not mean to cause so much trouble!"

"Then why did you choose to jump onto that dangerous trawler, Master Kitty?" Mrs. Owl leans forward and quietly waits for the answer.

"Well, er, I, I guess, uh, I made a bad decision. I think I should have thought more first. Is that right, Mrs. Owl?"

"Yes. We make better decisions when we think things over first, Master Kitty. Please keep thinking about it."

"I will." Kitty seriously replies. To think, however, I need food, meow!"

Max looks at Sara and then at Mr. and Mrs. Owl. "He is going to stinking forget as soon as he gets to his food bowl, isn't he?"

The End

A Kitty Adventure

A book series about the life of Kitty

A NOTE FROM THE AUTHOR

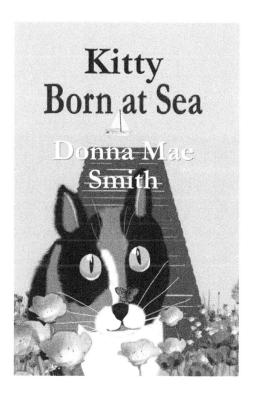

Kitty Born at Sea: A KITTY ADVENTURE #1 is Kitty's first adventure. He lives aboard the big boat, Betty, and sails from Mexico to Virginia with Momma, Captain, and Rod. Read about Kitty and his many adventures while growing up at sea.

Please offer our books a review at any of your favorite book sites. Reviews help us gain a larger audience!

Links to Kitty's books: DonnaMaeSmith.com

Contact us: Donna@DonnaMaeSmith.com

    Kitty@DonnaMaeSmith.com

Interact and get to know us! facebook.com/AKittyAdventure

We like friends!

Made in the USA
Monee, IL
19 April 2023

32130173R00095